Immortal Evelyn
And Other Tales of Dark Fantasy

JEFFREY LYMAN

PAPER PHOENIX PRESS

Pennsville, NJ

PUBLISHED BY

eSpec Books LLC
Danielle McPhail, Publisher
PO Box 242,
Pennsville, New Jersey 08070
www.especbooks.com

ISBN: 978-1-965266-05-2
ISBN (eBook): 978-1-965266-04-5

Cover and Interior Design: Danielle McPhail, McP Digital Graphics

Illustrations: Art Credits - www.shutterstock.com
Fantasy woman queen with metallic golden skin © Ironika

To my wonderful wife, Angel,
and amazing sons, Eddie and Austin.

Contents

Cauterize the Wound

Professor Solomon Van Eyck entered the College of the Atheneum Illustre one bitter, January morning to find his demonstration cadaver missing. None of the professors would admit to the absence, and his interrogation of the cleaning staff elicited nothing further. The woman's corpse had been on the table when the doors were locked the night before. Now it was gone.

Standing in the lecture pit beside the empty table he clenched his fists, looking up at the seats above him. The students' pranks had gotten out of hand and something needed to be done. He had better not find the body in a closet somewhere, or worse, violated. Though perhaps a case of syphilis was what the perpetrators deserved.

Furious, he strode to the offices of the Rector Magnificus, Professor Dr. Willem Moll, in the Agnietenkapel. Professor Moll rose from his desk with a smile as Solomon entered, obviously delighted by some news.

"Professor Van Eyck," Professor Moll bellowed, his smile broadening further. "I believe that we are well on our way to transforming the Atheneum Illustre into a University. Won't that be wonderful? It may only be a few years now. *The University of Amsterdam.*" He spoke proudly. It had long been his dream to make the Atheneum into a true rival of the University of Leiden.

Solomon bowed, honoring decorum before voicing his grievances. "You have been our college master for twenty-three years, Professor Moll. It will be an honor to see you university master."

Professor Moll tossed aside the missive that delighted him so, perhaps one more letter of support from the city fathers. "But that is not why you come to me, Professor Van Eyck. What can I do for you?"

"Someone," Solomon stated, "has stolen my cadaver. I must have a subject for my lecture, which is to start momentarily." Both men looked out the window at the tower-clock across the square. It read ten minutes until the hour.

"That is, indeed, serious," Professor Moll replied. "We will find you a suitable replacement immediately and make further inquiries afterward."

And thus Solomon had the unpleasant task of sharing a corpse with Professor Hoogh, who would be lecturing on the bowel system in the afternoon and so had not disturbed the circulatory system of the arms, which Solomon was reviewing.

A more thorough search in the afternoon failed to produce the missing cadaver, so he was forced to work late preparing another subject. He refused to share a body with Professor Hoogh two days in a row. Not with bowels everywhere.

The new corpse, an otherwise healthy pauper who had sold his body to the College for quick money, had died in a fall the day before. Solomon worked quickly and precisely with his scalpels, peeling back swatches of skin to expose the major veins and arteries, all the while nursing his anger at this waste of his time. He tried to ignore the faint scratching of rats, so much like fingernails, back below the raised seats. *Wherever there are bodies there are rats,* he told himself. He hated rats. Vermin. Their bites were so infectious. Their teeth sharp. He shivered.

Eventually the constant noises got to him, and he walked to the small access door, low on the wall of his teaching pit. It led to the crawlspace below the student seats, and he had checked it earlier to make sure that the pranksters hadn't stuffed the missing body there. They couldn't have taken her far. Carrying around a dead, naked prostitute was hardly inconspicuous. Especially a body that had gone through two lectures under his scalpel.

He yanked open the access door and stuck his head through, thrusting his candle into the void.

"Hey!" he shouted. The scratching stopped, replaced by the scurrying of tiny feet from deeper in the darkness. The candle illuminated a few feet, a couple of wooden supports, dust, spider webs. Rats and confining places! Two things he loathed.

He examined again the dust of the floor just inside the door. It had been disturbed. He hadn't seen it earlier in his anger and urgency to find a replacement body. He looked more closely. The scuff marks didn't bear the hallmarks of crawling boys dragging a corpse, but someone, for some reason, had been in here. He dipped the candle back and forth, examining the dust. Well, they would not make him the butt of their jokes in his own lecture hall!

He pushed forward into the cold, stale air of the space, and immediately his breathing grew faster, loud in the muffled darkness. He had to control his body. There was nothing to fear here. Just rats and maybe the corpse of a prostitute. He lifted his right knee to bring his leg through the door and ran straight into a spider web. Sputtering and sneezing and slapping at his face, he backed out and slammed the door. It was late and he should be at home. His son needed him more than ever these days with the sickness. The cleaning staff could look under the seats tomorrow.

On his way out, he stopped by Professor Broen's office and knocked softly.

"How many today?" he asked softly when invited inside.

"Three new cases with mild symptoms," Professor Broen said, "and two more bodies in our morgue. Don't worry, Solomon. We'll find a cure." Solomon nodded and took his leave, going to hail a carriage home.

Nothing is incurable, he told himself over and over on his ride home. *Nothing is beyond the minds of such men as are gathered in the Atheneum Illustre and the University of Leiden.*

It took him a long time to fall asleep, and when he finally slept he was restless. He awoke in deep darkness; certain he had heard something. He lifted his head—loathe to expose his skin to the freezing night air — and peered around his bedroom, listening. The moon had set, and the room looked like a faint etching on gray slate. Nothing moved. No sound repeated itself, but something had awakened him.

Elizabeth stirred in her sleep beside him and pulled the blankets tighter around her throat. He looked over at his wife of twenty-four years. Her black hair, now striped with gray, was tangled around her head. "Rest easy, Elizabeth. I'll be back."

Frigid January air oozed in through the gaps and cracks of their old house; her father's house. He swung his legs over the edge of the bed and shivered violently until he could wrap a heavy woolen robe around himself. He pulled his nightcap down tighter over his ears. Fortunately, the iron bed-warmer below the bed remained hot enough to have kept his slippers warm. God, it was cold! It burned his nose when he breathed.

He grabbed a candle nub from his desk and lit it from the embers of the fireplace. The pages for tomorrow's lecture lay ghostly on the black-lacquered desktop. *My new cadaver had better be there when I arrive in the morning,* he thought in a flash of irritation, a carryover from the day.

The floorboards creaked under his feet as he checked on Marya. His daughter was still asleep. Lawrence, his son, recently home from medical school, was not in his bed. Solomon grew immediately concerned.

The talk of Amsterdam lately had been of nothing but this new *sleeping disease* that Solomon feared was taking Lawrence. It had claimed dozens of victims in the last two months — death being preceded by increasing exhaustion, anemia, and hallucinations. His demonstration cadaver, the prostitute who had gone missing, was one of the victims.

Solomon hoped his son's condition was just a lack of energy brought on by the cold and darkness of winter. Nevertheless, he kept lengthy notes on Lawrence's condition and plied him with every herb or powder he could think of or that Professor Broen suggested.

The professors at both the Atheneum and the University of Leiden still hunted for a cause, methodically yet with growing urgency. The theologians were equally busy seeking signs of God's displeasure. And though Solomon mocked them, the theologians were having more success. They blamed the Jewish refugees who had been streaming into the city from Antwerp over the last few years.

On top of this sickness that had everyone pestering the hospitals or crowding the churches, a dozen men had been discovered in various parts of the city with their throats cut and their bodies drained of blood. The police had been unable to apprehend this bizarre killer, and these two items dominated the gossip of the fashionable circles. It was lucky that the winter was so unnaturally cold. The populace didn't have the energy to panic.

Solomon proceeded downstairs, his breath billowing as clouds of steam, and stopped as he rounded the final corner of the staircase. The fire in the parlor had been built up.

"Who's there?" Solomon demanded sternly. "Lawrence?"

Father," came a rasp from one of the two wing-backed chairs facing the fire. "I'm sorry to have awakened you."

Solomon strode forward and skirted the chair. When he saw his son he gasped, nearly dropping his candle. Lawrence was as pale as snow, his lips a faint slash between sunken cheeks. His eyes were swollen, with great, dark circles beneath them. His hair was wild from the pillow, and Solomon could swear there was more gray in it than a month ago when he first returned home. "Are you all right?"

"I couldn't sleep," Lawrence whispered, fingering a heavy, gold cross around his neck, about four inches tall, suspended from an ornate, double-interlocked, gold chain. "I dreamed of a great moth fluttering at my window."

Solomon had not raised his son to believe in superstitions. "Lawrence, where did you get that?"

Lawrence met his eyes for a moment, and then glanced down at the cross. "The jeweler's shop at the corner of the Market Square."

"Why?"

Lawrence smiled. "I'm dying, Father." Solomon winced. "I have the *sleeping disease*," he continued. "I am exhausted, and yet I don't sleep. The sleep I do find is populated with nightmares."

"There will be a cure." Solomon was convinced of it. "Don't worry. The greatest minds of the city are working on it."

"Perhaps the theologians are correct, and God is punishing us."

"God has no place in science!"

Lawrence chuckled, then winced as he slipped the cross gingerly out of sight under his robe.

Solomon duly noted his son's weakness as the young man closed his eyes for a moment and clenched his jaw. He would write it down later in his journal. As well as this sudden interest in religion. Perhaps it was worse than he feared. Lawrence was slipping into the final stage of the disease—the end stage punctuated by hallucinations.

Not speaking, Lawrence struggled to his feet, keeping his hand protectively against the cross. "I am returning to bed," he wheezed. He began to limp toward the stairs and Solomon stepped up next to him. Lawrence gripped his father's shoulder tightly for strength. "I understand that the marvels of our age have made you a devout atheist, Father," Lawrence whispered, "but in my time in medical school, I saw things that convinced me otherwise."

Solomon laughed, though he tried not to, and Lawrence grimaced.

"I am sorry, Lawrence, but God is a tale your grandparents told you as a baby. This is the age of wonders, and it is best to let superstitions die."

"They say there is an unholy beast at the source of this plague."

Solomon shook his head, saddened. "You've been listening to gossip. That is not proper for a young man of your standing."

"They say he was a man once, and that he sold his soul to the Devil."

"Like Dr. Johannes Faustus?"

"Not like Faust. This thing had no need of gold or relics in exchange for his soul."

"What then?"

Lawrence stopped and looked at his father. "Immortality."

"Immortality? Now what would the Devil gain by such a compact?"

"This man would never go to Hell. The Devil could never collect." Lawrence started up the stairs. "The gifts of Satan come with a price. It is rumored that if the man, this *thing*, cannot continue killing, then he has failed in his half of the bargain. His soul will be forfeit. They say it is a hunger in him."

"And you believe this fantasy is at the heart of your sleeplessness and nightmares?"

"Not all killers leave a mark."

Solomon forced himself to keep silent as he and his son slowly mounted the stairs. It was absurd, thinking a murderer could cause sleeplessness and anemia. The public was desperate for a cause. But everything would be fine. Solomon remained confident in this.

As they parted at Lawrence's door, Solomon's son met his eyes. "Faust was saved in the end by Gretchen. Perhaps this beast will one day return to the light at the hand of a woman." And then he closed his bedroom door.

"You're cold," Elizabeth murmured as Solomon climbed back into bed beside her, and she moved away from him. He didn't tell her of his conversation with Lawrence. Their son's weakening condition upset her terribly. He blew out his candle and stared into blackness. Immortality! Foolishness, though he could see the attraction in such fairy tales. Death was an ending like the quenching of a flame. To cheat it was a wonderful fantasy indeed.

Traveling to the Atheneum by coach in the following morning's darkness, Solomon marveled at the frozen canals. He had rarely seen them freeze so hard in his life. The children, on their way to work in the factories, were playing games on the ice; trying to chase each other but falling instead. He had not wanted children originally, and had only had two at Elizabeth's insistence. He found he liked them more than he had expected.

Such sentimentality was unbecoming, he knew, but there it was. And it clouded every thought he had about the sleeping sickness. So much so that he made a detour to the morgue before going to his lecture hall. No new bodies had been brought in during the night. He walked between the older ones laid in rows on the tables—men and women and children, frozen and lifelike even days after death.

His new cadaver was still in the lecture hall when he arrived, so the irritation he had been brooding over cooled a bit. He attempted one more cursory look for the missing body, but only stared at the door to the underside of the seats before turning away. He would wait until after the thaw. Then the prostitute would be easily located from her stink.

He finished preparing the new body just as his students trooped in, and continued his lecture on the circulatory systems with his hands dappled with blood. He used his scalpel like a pointer, speaking up to his students in the bleachers. The rats below the seats were, for the most part, quiet today.

He rushed home as quickly as he could in the later afternoon and sought his son immediately. Lawrence was sitting in a chair against the wall with his eyes closed. Elizabeth murmured, "He didn't sleep well last night, so he took laudanum and slept the day away. He is only recently up and about." She looked up into Solomon's eyes, worry and fear stamped across her face. "Is he going to be all right?"

"He'll be fine," Solomon grunted. When she continued to stare, he drew her into his arms. "He is ill, Elizabeth, but we're working on a cure. He'll be fine."

When she reluctantly left, he drew a chair near to where his son dozed. Lawrence's thick hair hung lank around his head, and his necktie hung loose. He opened his eyes, and it seemed to Solomon that the draught of laudanum had not yet run its course.

"How do you feel today?" Solomon waited as Lawrence attempted to sit up straight.

"I'll live. Thank you for your help last night. Without you I would have slept the night near the fire."

"I want to talk to you about that while dinner is being prepared. You spoke a great deal of foolishness last night, and I don't want you upsetting your mother and sister. Your mother is worried enough without tales of beasts and compacts with the Devil."

Lawrence didn't reply for a long while, but eventually said, "I may have spoken too freely and I apologize. I won't repeat myself in front of Mother."

Solomon remained stern. "And this demon who preys on our city?"

Lawrence sat up straighter. "I know, I should not listen to gossip. It is unbecoming for a young man of my station." And then he slouched back down.

Solomon nodded. He left him there and retired to his desk while the preparations for dinner continued. Tomorrow's lecture would be a continuation of today's, wherein he would open the throat of the cadaver and demonstrate the tremendous vessels that transported blood to the brain—the center of thought. Man was a thinking animal, and Lawrence's fear of and belief in the supernatural was a primitive instinct that Solomon Van Eyck could not abide.

Additional Laudanum gave Lawrence another good night's sleep, and he felt well enough to accompany Solomon to the Atheneum the following morning. They parted company once inside, Solomon to his lecture hall, Lawrence to the morgue. Solomon had told him of the bodies down there, and Lawrence was keen to help in the investigation of a cure, though he previously hadn't had the energy.

Between morning and afternoon lectures, Solomon stopped by the morgue to see how his son was getting on. The mortician told him with a thinly disguised smirk that Lawrence had left after just an hour.

"And why is that funny?" Solomon demanded.

"Nothing, Professor Van Eyck. I've just never seen a graduate of the medical school who was so weak-stomached at the sight of a corpse before."

"My son is not weak stomached!" He wasn't. The boy had never been put off by anything.

"Of course, of course, professor. But our coterie of poor souls here certainly had him upset."

Solomon finished his afternoon lectures in a distracted state, certain later that he had missed several important veins.

Dinner that night was mutton stew, as it was every Tuesday, and Elizabeth and the children made small talk. Solomon didn't join in. He watched his son. The young man certainly ate heartily enough, but soon after excused himself to his bedroom. After dinner, Solomon mounted the stairs and knocked quietly on Lawrence's door.

"Yes?" came the muffled response, and Solomon turned the knob and entered. Lawrence was sitting on the edge of his bed in his nightclothes, shivering, staring out of his bedroom windows at the dark night.

"Did you see something?" Solomon asked, stepping up to the diamond-paned glass and looking down on the street below. Along the way, someone dressed in heavy furs hustled along before turning off onto a side street. It was another cold night. Would January never end?

"No, nothing," Lawrence replied, but his voice remained distant.

Solomon went to him and met his eyes, examining his face. His son was barely awake. He might have fallen asleep sitting there and frozen to death. "Into bed," Solomon ordered, and Lawrence complied. Solomon checked that the bed warmer was still giving off plenty of heat.

"You didn't remain long this morning at the college," he said.

Lawrence shuddered. "All those bodies. I couldn't look at them."

"They're just bodies."

"They looked so alive."

"Yes, I know. They all died of extremely low blood levels, and some have theorized that decomposition has been delayed by this lack of a fluid medium in the body. I think it's just the cold."

"No, it's not the cold." Lawrence's voice grew fainter, and Solomon stepped forward to hear. "I felt like they were still alive, just sleeping. I thought I could hear a blackbird caged by the ribs of each, struggling to break free. It was horrifying. I couldn't listen to that pecking and fluttering any longer."

Solomon ground his teeth. The situation grew worse. He feared that Lawrence couldn't survive many more days. He would have to talk to Elizabeth tonight. Prepare her. He closed his eyes. How could he prepare her? How could he prepare himself? His son wasn't supposed to die. There had to be a way to save him.

He placed his hand on his son's head for a moment before turning to leave, but Lawrence reached up and gripped his wrist weakly. "Science won't explain away all mysteries, Father," he whispered.

"Lawrence!" Solomon was insulted. How dare his son criticize the science that Solomon Van Eyck based his life on?

"I am sorry, Father, but sometimes belief in something larger is the only path to the truth."

"Deliberate research and the scientific method succeed where superstitions will always fail."

"No." Lawrence opened his eyes. "Listen to me. I have been thinking on the gossip you hate. I wondered how this demon-man could have gotten access to me. I did not remember permitting anyone into our home. Then I recalled the foreign Prince."

Solomon frowned. "What is this?"

"Prince Leonid Nikolayevitch Barashkov, of Petrograd. When he and his grandfather first arrived in Amsterdam, he made the rounds of the noble families. It was during the day, so you were at the college."

"I remember your mother mentioning that." Elizabeth's family was of the noble class, so they occasionally had foreign noblemen introducing themselves.

"He frightened me, though I don't know why. I have dreamed of him several times since then. Maybe he is the demon itself, or an emissary preparing the way."

"That is nonsense. Go to sleep and don't dwell on such dire thoughts."

It only took a moment for Lawrence to fall into the breathing patterns of sleep, and Solomon watched for signs of nightmares. Nothing. His son was at peace. As he turned to go, he caught sight of the gold cross around Lawrence's neck. Determined to prove to his son that this was all nonsense, he gently removed it and dropped it into his pocket. Such trinkets were not necessary for a good night's rest.

A short while later, his daughter Marya retired to her room for the night. Solomon waited in the parlor for everything to quiet down with impatience, because it was Tuesday, the night he and Elizabeth always made love. They had mutton stew on Tuesday, and they made love. It had been so ever since they were married. Tonight he would talk to her about Lawrence instead. He just needed to think of the words. She would weep, and he might too.

He sat in one of the winged-back chairs in front of the fire, warming his toes and allowing his scarf to slip from his throat. He had gotten down one of the medical texts of Galen, hoping that the Greek master physician might have listed an illness with similar symptoms to their current scourge. Something to save Lawrence. Others had read through the books already, but Van Eyck's knowledge of Greek was superior to his fellow professors. In Latin he was their equal, but he excelled at Greek.

Elizabeth, descending the stairs, said, "It is time for bed, Solomon."

Solomon looked up at her. He loved her very much. He struggled for the words. "Elizabeth, we need to talk about Lawrence."

She froze at the bottom of the steps. "Talk about what, Solomon? You said he would be fine."

"Elizabeth, we are racing toward a cure, but I don't know that we will be in time." A tightness in his throat threatened to choke off his words. "We have not spoken of this aloud, but it is the *sickness*. I can't deny it any longer."

She paled, still standing at the bottom of the steps. Her hands clung together. "You said he would be fine." Her voice trembled and the tightness in his own throat grew worse. She turned and ran up the steps.

"Elizabeth!" Solomon leapt up and raced after her. He reached her just as she grasped the doorknob of Lawrence's bedroom and the door swung inward. The first thing that Solomon noticed was that the room was freezing. He couldn't figure out why Lawrence would have opened his windows.

Elizabeth bustled forward and pulled the windows shut, almost losing them for a moment as a gust of wind tried to snatch them from her hands.

Solomon looked down at his son. Lawrence lay placidly under a mound of blanket, eyes closed and darkly ringed like a badger's. Suddenly he sensed that something vital had gone from the boy; some spark had faded. That realization startled him. Until this moment he had thought of the terminus of life like a gas lamp as it is shut off: no flicker, no afterglow, just an end and then darkness. But staring down at Lawrence, it didn't feel like that. It felt like a tide pouring back into a vast sea, leaving behind the smooth, washed sand. *He's dead*, he thought, stunned. *He's not breathing*.

"I can't imagine how these windows got open," Elizabeth whispered.

"Elizabeth," Solomon choked. He sat on the edge of the bed and took his son's cold hand.

"What?" She put her hand to her mouth in silent horror, and then ran to her boy. "No," she howled, the tears coming. "You said he would be fine!"

"I just left him an hour ago." Tears glazed his eyes. "He *was* fine. He was sleeping peacefully."

"What is it?" Marya said from the door. She ran to her mother. Solomon wiped his eyes. It was too soon. His boy was dead too soon.

The professors and doctors had not been fast enough. They had failed. He felt hollow, like the moment after the orchestra stops playing and silence falls.

He staggered to the recently closed window. Movement caught his eye. Down below, in the winter street lit by gas lamps, a man in a top hat and cloak walked away down the center of the street. Behind him dragged a shadow of something not man-shaped. It billowed and rippled like a sheet in the wind.

"What *is* that?" Solomon shook his head and wiped his eyes again. Sometimes the gas lamps distorted shadows.

He looked to his boy and then back out to the now empty street, his anger finally beginning to fill the nothingness that had eaten away his internal organs. Elizabeth cradled Lawrence in her arms, rocking and moaning softly. Solomon welcomed her keening. Silence was worse. He rubbed his arms. He didn't know how to grieve. He wanted to sob like his daughter, but he could not.

He lifted Lawrence's cross from his pocket and fingered the edges.

Such a small thing.

He clenched his teeth, remembering the fairy tales his mother had once told him. The power of the supernatural would be greatest in the night but could be held at bay with religious icons. Had he killed Lawrence by taking this cross?

He dropped it back into his pocket. No. The disease was just a disease.

Solomon Van Eyck walked into the College of the Atheneum Illustre just as the sun rose. He had not slept but had stayed with Elizabeth while she held Lawrence. The morticians had come now and were transforming the front parlor to hold Lawrence's body for the wake.

Solomon couldn't watch them. He had gripped the cross in his pocket and numbly answered questions directed to him until he'd had to flee the house. Grief now completely filled the place where science and probability used to dwell, and that grief had not abated on his long, cold walk to the College. He wouldn't be able to do his lectures today. He would have to tell Rector Magnificus Moll.

As he walked down the cold and echoing hallway of the Atheneum, the college mortician hurried past him, obviously angry. The man stopped short as he recognized Solomon. "Your cadaver was stolen, wasn't it?"

"Did you find it?"

"Two more bodies went missing from the mortuary last night. Rector Moll is terribly upset. He has called an assembly of the boys for eight o'clock. We cannot allow these pranks to continue."

"No, we can't," Solomon said absently. He didn't really care right now if the boys were stealing bodies.

Standing in his lecture pit beside his latest body, he touched the cold, semi-hard skin. Lawrence's hand had felt like this last night. Faint light descended from high clerestory windows above, but gloom still draped the pit. Solomon lit a candle.

The scurrying claws of rats below the seats distracted him, so he strode to the small access door on the wall and pulled it open. He thrust the lantern out in the dark void.

"Hey!" The scratching hesitated for a moment in the gloom then began again.

Solomon forced his shoulders in, and then his legs, and crawled through thick cobwebs and dust, waving the candle about. Cobwebs didn't matter. There was something in here and he needed to see it with his own eyes. Lawrence's gold cross hung heavy in his pocket.

He prayed that she wouldn't be here; that science and reason still mattered. But no. She was there. In the far recesses of the crawl space he found his missing cadaver.

A young, naked prostitute surrounded by dozens of rat corpses. Her left arm terminated at the elbow, the white end of the humerus glistening in his candle's light. He himself had removed her forearm not three days before to demonstrate the vessels running through the joint. A tremendous patch of skin was missing from her inner thigh where he had presented the femoral artery. In all parts of her body the skin and muscle had been peeled away by his scalpel. She was a patchwork doll, and she glared at him with an evil fury.

His anger flickered and then rose to meet hers.

Crippled, she lurched at him. He snapped free one of the smaller wooden boards of the seating structure. Equally calmly, determined, and methodical, he slashed at her main arteries and veins with the broken end of the board, pushing her back as she rabidly tried to advance.

She had been empty of blood when she died. He reasoned that a need to replace her blood had brought her back. The vascular system was her weakness. He slashed the stick across her throat, and she fell.

She lay on her side, staring up at him with animal confusion, her throat hanging open. She was no longer capable of attack. He crawled close and drove the stick between her ribs and into her heart, quieting her eyes.

Then he sat back against a post and truly cried. Tears fell and froze on his collar. He had to get home to his parlor where even now Lawrence was being laid out in his best suit. His son couldn't be allowed to return like this, crouched in a hole and eating rats. Solomon needed to go, but he couldn't yet make himself move.

He gazed at the prostitute, her dull eyes the proper filmy shade for death, her hair matted and dirty. Her destruction had been a mercy. So would Solomon's desecration of Lawrence's body. There would be others across the city — including the ones down in the Atheneum morgue. He must cauterize the wound before it turned gangrenous.

Lawrence had told him; had warned him! He had even given a name — Prince Barashkov. Solomon would visit the prince's home. Perhaps this man was the source of the scourge. He lifted the cross from his pocket and hung it around his neck.

Then he stopped. Perhaps Lawrence had been too far gone in his hallucinations and it was just a disease after all, albeit a peculiar one not yet explained.

Solomon had failed his son because he had refused to consider something that defied logic and reason. But just because it could not be explained, did not mean that it had to be supernatural. Solomon simply lacked the language to describe it. Even as he destroyed the victims of the disease, he would study them. He would solve this mystery.

This was the Age of Reason! There was no place for a supernatural explanation for this prostitute or for Prince Barashkov, certainly not that of a Faustian bargain. But it could stand as a preliminary hypothesis. Science would explain and illuminate the remainder.

Solomon lifted his lantern high and crawled back toward the distant hatchway.

Down on the Playground

The gray, sullen orphan
of decorated joy and longing,
waits in silence for the dance to end.

Like a distant fire on a dark prairie.
Like snow in April.

Elsi Latchka curled up at the head of her assigned bed, knees drawn up, headphones on, Iron Maiden loud, eyes closed. Not moving. Hoping her cocoon of darkness and white noise would hold. But no matter how hard she tried; she couldn't drown out the uneasy chattering of the dead. The voices grew louder every day while the doctors purged her system of old medications.

She hated the drugs and hated that she needed them, but she desperately hoped the doctors would find a new, working combination soon so she could go home. She had voluntarily come to the hospital after freaking out at work, but she didn't like being here longer than she had to.

She was twenty-five, with deep-set eyes and a shock of black hair that betrayed her Slavic ancestry. During the last five years of being in and out of hospitals, Elsi had vacillated between believing in ghosts and believing they were paranoid hallucinations. She was perfectly sane when she was on her drugs. She could hold down a job and keep an apartment. When the drugs inevitably lost their efficacy, she saw and felt things no one else did, thing that could see her back. Then she didn't believe they were hallucinations. Every night she stared at the ceiling in the dark and told herself it wasn't real.

Someone shouted her name, and she tugged off her headphones. "What?"

"C'mon, Elsi! We don't have all day to wait on you!" Mr. Al-Ahmed stuck his head and one shoulder through her doorway and glared. Her roommate, creepy, silent Mary, was already gone. Elsi threw aside the headphones and made herself move, because if she didn't, he would drag her out and she couldn't stand to be touched. She shoved her feet into her sneakers, crossed her arms and tucked her hands in tight, then scuttled past him into the corridor. He held the door for her.

The rest of her group was lined up in the monotonously off-white corridor that the psychiatric hospital seemed to think was soothing.

"Let's go," called Mrs. Sanders cheerfully from the front, and the twenty residents shuffled forward. Participation in group activities was mandatory, and every other day meant a trip outside. Elsi kept her head down. She'd have bolted back to her room if she thought she could get away with it. She had tried it before. She was terrified of the outside, because outside was where Junior waited.

"He's a hallucination," she mumbled as she walked down the corridor. "He's just a hallucination." As usual, the walls around her thrummed and whispered. No one else noticed. If the ghosts knew Elsi could see and hear them they would come by the thousands, with all of their pent-up anger and fears. She was blindingly terrified of ever being swarmed again.

"It's just a hallucination. It's not real."

The group descended two floors to a back door with heavy-gage security mesh over the window and walked through. Maribel, ahead of Elsi in line, shoved the door open with a bang. Elsi, arms still tightly crossed, dodged through after her without touching anything. Jessi behind her shoved it open with another bang.

"Freak," Jessi muttered, glaring at Elsi. As if she should talk. Jessi had wet herself again, evidenced by a spot on the back of her sundress and the smell of urine.

Elsi descended the steps to the cracked and undulous blacktop she liked to call *The Playground*, though there were no swings. A nine-foot-high security fence surrounded the yard, and basketball hoops hung from lightly canted poles at the ends. Beyond this fenced-in pen lay staff parking and a small pond, infested with Canada geese. The sky above was a billowing mat of gray and darker gray, too thick to show the sun.

The other *nuthatches* spread out from the back door into the playground. One of the attendants threw a basketball out and it hit the ground with a 'pang' of rubber on blacktop. Outdoor-time lasted an hour and to Elsi it was fifty-nine minutes too long. A dozen ghosts and indeterminate blotches wandered in agitation across the open space.

And there was Junior.

He sat in the center of the playground: a child digging with a little, yellow, beach shovel. He terrified her more than any ghost she had ever seen, and she was plenty scared of them all. He wore a polo shirt with horizontal black and red stripes and a great big collar, circa 1979. A mop of thick, brown hair humped out over his ears. Day after day he dug, and tunelessly hummed TV-show theme songs.

Elsi couldn't look at him. She knew what he looked like from peripheral vision and from quick, sliding glances, but that was enough. He was different from the other wispy ghosts and lingering memories. He squatted in the center of the playground like a cannonball on a bed, pulling everything else toward him. The pavement seemed to tilt so badly that Elsi felt like she stood on a hillside. No one else noticed this dramatic weight in their midst.

She held out a trembling hand and tried to steady it. She hadn't always been crazy but five years ago, she and a bunch of college friends had tried to see ghosts. Desmond screwed up the magic spell. Desmond cursed them all because he said he knew old French, the stupid prick, and he screwed it up. He read it wrong, or he got the ingredients wrong, or whatever! Elsi kicked at a pebble, and then froze up as it skittered toward the voracious abyss of Junior. She relaxed a little when the pebble stopped, and Junior kept digging.

The doctors insisted he couldn't exist. They said there were no ghosts, and there couldn't have been magic that windy afternoon because magic isn't real. Desmond couldn't have screwed it up. It was in Elsi's head. Her damaged head. The doctors agreed she had given herself brain damage after too much coke and too many other drugs during a week-long bender leading up to the magic spell. Yeah, that was it. Brain damage. Junior was a symptom. A really heavy symptom that wanted to drag her in.

She stepped aside as an elderly black man in a stained and battered trucker's cap that said *#1 Granddad* on the front descended the steps with Mr. Al-Ahmed. Milford always came last. "Seven, eight, nine," he muttered to himself. He was counting cracks. For half of their time outdoors, Milford would count his way slowly out from the steps. Then an attendant would shout, "It's time, Milford," and Milford would count his way back in. He often confided in people that if he could reach the far fence, he would be cured. Elsi had never seen him make it halfway across. There were too many cracks. And yet he diligently made his laborious escape attempt every other day. They said he'd been trying for years.

Elsi glanced up at the tumbling sky and then began to walk the right side of the perimeter. She couldn't remain motionless. She couldn't let her stupid hallucinations find her standing still. Her right shoulder brushed the wires of the fence, as far from the center of the playground as she could get. Far from Junior. She shivered, and the shiver ran up and down her spine until she could mash down her panic. Damn it! Stupid Desmond and his stupid magic spell.

Elsi pretended not to hear the voices as she walked. Right here, they whispered, right on this spot where she stood/passed/moved on, old Willem Olfsson had attempted to escape on June 14, 1972, at 6:27 in the evening. He blamed his failure on his bum leg, which allowed the attendants to catch him just as he grasped the wires of the fence, just as his fingertips tasted sweet freedom. An attendant named John Astor, who outweighed Willem Olfsson by 150 pounds and had six inches of height on him, kicked him in the back of the legs to bring him to the ground. Willem struck his head on this very blacktop that had not been repaved since and died.

John Astor, killed in a fall two years later, defended himself in Elsi's left ear. He insisted, as he had in the inquiry after the Olfsson incident, that he had merely stopped Willem from climbing the fence. Willem was seventy-eight. John was twenty-four. Elsi ignored these bickering remnants and kept walking. She had heard them every other fucking day for the last several weeks, and knew their fight would never end. They were incapable of reconciliation or change. As she suspected she might be. Most days she felt as trapped in the static, angry world of the dead as they were.

Willem Olfsson wasn't much of a ghost, as far as ghosts went. He was an imprint of an event; a place memory of something bad that had happened. John Astor had more solidity. He was an emotional imprint, constantly trying to justify himself. He had probably started out haunting the stairwell where he met his end but had instinctively migrated to Willem's constant recycling of that day. They were binary stars now, circling each other and fading as the years passed.

She turned at the fence-corner and walked along the far side parallel to the parking lot. Her roommate, Mary Dougal, stood sentinel at the next corner. Scarred and silent Mary. She had been at the hospital for almost three weeks now, a few days shorter than Elsi, but she hadn't spoken more than a dozen words since arriving. Mary turned her head and looked at Elsi and then turned away.

Mary was in her mid-twenties like Elsi, and her hair and eyes were the exact same shade of brown. Her gaze always seemed to be directed toward the horizon. She had a thin, austere elegance that might have been beautiful if not for the damage. Burn scarring clutched the right side of her neck, throat, and jaw, wrapping behind her ear and disappearing under her hair. She wore long-sleeved shirts, and her right hand was hidden in a tight, leather driving glove. She usually kept it tucked against her stomach. When she walked, she limped.

"Watch'a looking at, Mary?" Elsi asked, but didn't slow down because she knew Mary wouldn't answer. Elsi usually tried to get her to talk. Sometimes she tried a joke; sometimes she was rude. She turned the corner, heading back toward the door, the stairs, and the building.

"How's it going, Elsi?"

Elsi looked up at the man's voice, high and rough. Director Zirkowski stood on the other side of the fence, a McDonald's bag in his hand. He was about fifty-five, she guessed, and had stopped buying new pairs of glasses sometime twenty years ago. They were easily four times as big as the oval lenses she wore. At least he knew her name. That counted for something.

"My bra-strap broke this morning, and nobody had a bra in my size to lend," she said. "We put it back together with duct-tape."

He was taken aback, as she meant for him to be. "Well, um, I'm sorry to hear that." He fidgeted and gave a weak smile.

Elsi watched him walk away, accompanied by a grim, older woman in gray tweed. A dead woman. Director Zirkowski had mother issues. Just as he had been unable to let her go upon her death, she had been unwilling to let him go. Elsi was careful to keep her eyes on the center of his back and not to acknowledge his mother.

She shook her head and continued on. To her left, Milford doggedly pursued his forward progress counting cracks. To her left, Junior dug.

When Elsi finished the circuit, Dr. Grossjean was waiting for her by the stairs. He was young and energetic, not yet burned out. He was always trying to get her to confront her fears, and she sometimes tried for him. He had an affable naiveté and optimism that was almost strong enough to make her believe him.

"Elsi," he said. He had his hands in his pockets, casual.

"Dr. Grossjean." She made herself stop.

"You're walking the fence again."

"I know." She couldn't meet his eyes.

"You did good on Tuesday. Let's see you walk out to Milford today."

Elsi looked at #1 Granddad. He wasn't that far. Maybe she could run to him and back with no ghosts the wiser. She looked at Dr. Grossjean and shook her head.

"Come on." He held out his hand. "I'll walk with you."

His might have been the only hand she would take when she was this jumpy. His palm was never sweaty, and he didn't grip too tightly. Sometimes, in the late afternoons before it got dark, she fantasized about him. "Okay," she said, and they started walking.

She took slow, baby-steps at first while he talked blithely about nothing and matched his pace with hers. She was panicky, and sought the anger that usually helped her function. Finally it came: frustration that she couldn't walk across an open blacktop; anger that Dr. Grossjean would never invite her out on a date because she was a patient to him; anger that she couldn't hold a job or keep friends or relate to her family. Stupid Desmond and his stupid magic spell. Her steps became bolder as she fought to defy her condition. Dr. Grossjean, bless him, kept talking and walking and not drawing attention to the struggle going on in her head. They passed Milford. She steered right, toward the fence, as the perceived slope of pavement became uncomfortable near Junior. She was proud of herself. She had come within fifteen feet of the little boy. Someday she would walk right past him.

She jerked her head up as the basketball bounced by her feet. She didn't have time to react as someone chasing the ball collided with Dr. Grossjean. He staggered into Elsi, and she was pushed right to the brink of Junior. She scuffed a little gravel over the edge into his hole. She sucked in her breath and balanced on the balls of her feet as that little, yellow shovel stopped scraping.

He raised his head, meeting her eyes. His irises were algae green, and there was blood swirling across the whites. The Canada geese in the pond behind the hospital took off in a thunder of wings.

Junior stood. He didn't come up higher than her waist, and yet she stood in his shadow. Her half-grasped convictions about hallucinations and all the courage she had borrowed from

Dr. Grossjean burned up and blew away. Junior opened his mouth and roared. Elsi fled, back to the stairs, fighting Mr. Al-Ahmed to get to the door. She kicked and punched. A second attendant grabbed her. They held her to the ground as she sobbed. A pinch against her upper arm signified the tranquilizer needle, but she was too far gone into the canyons of fear to stop clawing at the asphalt.

That night a storm blew in and rain rattled against the window. Elsi stared at the ceiling tiles in her room. They had given her some mild sedatives, but she still struggled against insomnia. She was embarrassed by her outburst earlier. A similar incident at work four weeks ago landed her in this place.

Dr. Grossjean sat down with her this evening after she woke from the tranquilizer. He had forced her to think logically about the incident. As frightening as Junior was, he hadn't actually done anything. Maybe he *was* just a hallucination like they said; the worst her brain and fears could come up with but incapable of harming her. Just maybe. She smiled a little.

She waited for Mary Dougal to drop off to sleep in the next bed. Then she slid out from between her hospital-issued sheets and padded to the window. She wanted it open to hear the rain.

She lifted the sliding window two inches, until it hit the suicide-stops. The smell of dampness and trees drifted in on little breezes. She hoped it would thunder; she craved noise to shush the uncomfortable spectral rumblings.

The clouds this afternoon had been like heavy wool, pressing in on her like a blanket, but cold; like something that wanted to comfort her but lacked the social skills to make a meaningful gesture. The sky was waiting for that moment when the pressure became too great and the clouds were squeezed like sponges, crying water in a tantrum.

Her love of storms went back much farther than the ghosts. She liked rain because she had always imagined herself sultry in gloom, alluring with her hair plastered down, shivering. In sunlight, she looked too pale and gaunt. In rain, with her wet, black clothes annealing to her skin, nipples on her small breasts hard, water falling from her fingertips as her hands hung lax at her sides, she could pretend. She could dare the boys to follow her out into the damp discomfort and control the moment because they stood on unfamiliar ground. Only once had she met a boy who liked rain as much as she, except he liked it for the experience of the absurd. He wanted to jump in puddles; she wanted to pull him down in the sodden grass. She wanted to feel the wet green on her back and the weight of him on her chest, and look up into the sky at the raindrops falling into her eyes. Two vastly different interpretations of what was essentially the same storm. How bizarre. She wondered if she was twisting what was pure, or he was. Still in all, she liked rain. Sunshine burned her eyes.

She glanced down onto the rain-blackened asphalt of the playground two stories below. The usual will-o-the-wisps and haunts fluttered about. For a moment she thought she saw that childhood boy again, but no, it was Junior, digging in his never expanding hole. Then he turned and looked up at her over his shoulder. She stepped back quickly, the soles of her feet cold on the vinyl floor tiles. Her heart sped up, fighting the sedatives.

He had looked at her! He was *aware* of her.

No, no, she thought, *He's a hallucination and my brain is making him scary*. She stepped forward again. She had to fight him to get better.

"I wouldn't do that, if I was you," came a rough voice from Mary's side of the room.

"What?" Elsi was stunned that Mary had spoken. Until that moment, Elsi hadn't quite thought of Mary as human. She was more like a scarred mannequin.

Mary sat up, groaning, and planted her feet on the floor, rubbing her face. "I need a cigarette," she said. "I haven't had one since I arrived. You don't have any, do you?"

"No," Elsi replied, aware that she was staring. "I don't smoke anymore."

"Ah well. As I was saying, don't piss off the child. It was asleep until you blundered into it today. Let it go back to sleep."

Elsi turned to the window, though she was still standing a pace back and so could only see the top of the far fence over the windowsill. A few hazy lights fluttered about the pond in the distance. "You can see him?"

"Yup."

"But he's a hallucination."

"Not this one." Mary stood and limped across the floor. Her cotton nightgown had sleeves. Elsi had seen her naked before, and she was burned up the whole right side of her body, like she'd been caught in an explosion. She came around to Elsi's right so that her unburnt arm was closest, and leaned forward a little to look out the window. She straightened. "I knew a few things once upon a time. That's how I got burnt, and so that time's over now. Try not to look at him for a couple of days."

Elsi was having trouble getting over the fact that Mary could see the little boy. Mary knew. That wasn't possible. "What is he?" She didn't want an answer.

"I couldn't say without talking to him, and I don't intend on doing that. As for the rest of them, you've got to learn to deal with them. Don't fight them so hard."

Elsi's mind snapped back to the three times she'd been swarmed by ghosts. She went numb. "There are too many of them," she whispered.

"I know, but you've got to make them obey you. Look right into their eyes and tell them to go away."

"I can't."

"Sure you can. You're strong. I would know."

"I can't do it." Elsi shuddered and clambered back into bed, the springs squealing under her weight. She wouldn't sleep tonight; not now. She was rigid with tension, tight from her ankles to her thighs to her stomach to her neck. She couldn't confront the ghosts.

Mary returned to her bed and pulled the sheets up to her chin. Her bedsprings were quiet.

"What about Junior?" Elsi had to ask. "Can I tell him to go away?"

"Not him. Let him sleep. If you let him be, he'll let you be. The rest, though. The rest will never let you be. You've got to fight them."

She tried to get Mary to talk the next day, but her roommate had lapsed back into silence. When they were led outside the day after that, Mary offered no support. She headed out to her usual post in the far corner to watch the world go by, walking through several ghosts on the way. Elsi heard her try to bum a cigarette off of an attendant, but he was talking on his cellphone and ignored her.

Elsi sat down on the top step by herself. Straight out from her knees was the withering cavern of Junior; the weight in the center of the sheet. She didn't look at him, but she could still hear him: the rhythmic, unceasing scrape of his little, yellow shovel in the dirt; his tuneless humming.

Dr. Grossjean came out about ten minutes later. He didn't offer her his hand and she kept hers tucked in tightly. Eventually, at his persistent encouragement, she resumed her circuit of the fence. By the second circuit, her anger began to return. Dr. Grossjean had dragged her out onto that blacktop and caused the subsequent encounter with Junior; Mary had told her to face her fears and then abandoned her like a platitude; stupid Desmond and his stupid magic spell! By the third circuit she was stamping her feet, hands shoved down into her pockets. She was fuming and walking fast when she nearly walked into someone at the far corner.

"Excuse me," she said without slowing.

"You can see me?"

She looked up into his eyes and knew him. George Abertine. He had died in 1857 of tuberculosis at the sanitarium that stood on the grounds of the current hospital. He was gaunt, far-gone in his illness. His eyes were feverish and glazed.

"You can see me." This time it was a statement and not a question.

Elsi recognized that now was the instant before the other ghosts caught on and swarmed. This was how it started. She clutched at the lifejacket Mary had tossed her two nights before. "Go away, George!" He was brought up short. "I said go away! You are dead. Everyone you know is dead. Why are you still here? Go home."

"You can see me." He sounded desperate.

"I can't see you." She focused her anger and walked away from him. He didn't follow. God help her, it had worked. The other ghosts hadn't had time to notice and the moment of swarming had passed. She walked on in elation, feeling nauseous.

On the next circuit she walked right by George Abertine. He didn't acknowledge her. He had already forgotten the incident, as she had hoped. He was so trapped in some personal moment or memory that no intrusion could hold his attention for long. She had beaten one of her hallucinations.

The next day the doctors started her on a new combination of meds, and the ghosts dropped away one by one. Most of her visual and auditory hallucinations faded to manageable levels: a rumble of background voices, cold spots, and flares of emotion. She could deal with those. Willem Olfsson and John Astor faded and she was glad to be done with them. George Abertine and other full apparitions lasted longer, and then they too faded. Junior, unfortunately, didn't. She was horrified to see him digging away after all the other ghosts had gone. How did he survive the deadening torpor of her new, powerful drugs?

She didn't tell the doctors about him when she demanded to be released. Dr. Grossjean would have liked to keep her longer, but the hospital let her go after three days of observation and extensive interviews. She wanted to get back to work and move on with her life.

Dr. Grossjean walked her to a waiting taxi on the morning of her release. She was so happy to be on the other side of the fence. It was outside-time again for her crew of twenty nuthatches. She passed Milford counting cracks, and urine-smelling Jessi.

She passed Junior and kept her eyes averted. She passed Mary Dougal at her corner-post, who nodded when Elsi said goodbye.

She climbed into the back seat of the taxi. The driver chatted with Dr. Grossjean as he tossed her suitcase into the trunk. She had a moment of bravery and decided to look at Junior. Mary had said to avoid him, but Elsi had begun to suspect that the whole late-night conversation with Mary had been a dream. She had been upset from the day and sedated, and Mary never spoke. The conversation had been Elsi's subconscious telling her how to handle her madness. Junior was just one more hallucination, albeit stronger than the rest. So she looked.

The instant she looked her chest collapsed into a cold, tight place that the mouse must feel when it sees the shadow of a hawk on the grass. Big shadow, little mouse.

Junior threw aside his yellow shovel and stood in dark blue jeans and dirty tennis shoes. His face twisted in anger. Driving forward, he loped toward her. The cracked and blistered asphalt below his feet rippled and bowed and shattered at each step. Elsi had only glimpsed the surface of how big he was. He was vast spaces and towering heights, folded and rolled into a tiny shell. Elsi panicked desperately. Why hadn't the taxi started? Why weren't they moving? Go! She clawed at the door handle, vaguely imagining herself trying to outrun this freight train coming across the grass.

Dr. Grossjean and the taxi driver looked at the ground. The car shook. The fence rattled. People around Junior teetered and wobbled, some fell. Earthquake! Elsi shrieked. But then Mary. She stepped out of her corner and threw a hard, left jab into Junior's mouth.

Silence. The earthquake halted mid-rumble. Junior lifted off of his feet and into the air, his head snapping back, his hair whipping into a halo. Mary stood half in a crouch, her fist still forward. Blood sprayed from Junior's torn lips, and he landed, splayed out and dazed. As he fell there came an aftershock, 4.6 on the Richter scale, the news said later.

"Did you feel that?" demanded the taxi driver. "An earthquake! We never get earthquakes around here." He stepped closer to the playground where half a dozen people were picking themselves up.

"Sometimes we do," Elsi breathed hard, staring through the open window. Mary straightened, blood dripping from her torn knuckles. Junior picked up his discarded shovel and returned to digging, only now his mouth bled into his hole and he was crying the great sobs of a child. Angry, petulant sobs.

Mary met Elsi's eyes and nodded. *I knew a few things, once upon a time.* Mary's words echoed in Elsi's memory. It was true, then. All real. The ghosts. Junior. The conversation. But who was Mary that she could beat down one of the dark ones digging at the weak points in the earth's crust? Who was she to possess such strength as that?

Elsi made herself climb out of the cab and walk to the woman. She put her fingers through the chain-link fence and held on, trembling. "Touch me," she said.

"You know I can't do that," Mary replied softly.

"Are you a ghost?"

"Not really." Mary looked out over the parking lot and pond as she did every day. "She's out there and she'll come for me someday."

Elsi looked in the direction Mary was looking, and then whipped back around, eyes wide, her heart speeding up in its old, familiar refrain. "You mean you're still alive?"

"Yes. Somewhere out there. We needed to be apart for a while to keep us safe, but now I can't find her."

Elsi backed away. Just as Junior was something new, so was Mary.

"You can't run forever, Elsi. Learn to control it, or it'll kill you. They'll kill you." Mary nodded toward Junior, then walked through the fence as if it wasn't there and headed out into the parking lot.

"You're leaving?"

"I wanted to help you a little bit. You're learning to control your gift, and when you can, help me find her. Please?"

"Who are you talking to, Elsi?" Dr. Grossjean stepped up beside her. He used his voice of fake concern.

"No one, doctor," Elsi replied, turning to face him. She couldn't let them send her back in there. She forced a calm veneer over her face. "I wanted to see if everyone was okay."

"Are you okay? You screamed."

"It was my first earthquake." She walked around him and climbed back into the cab. "I didn't like it." She didn't care if he believed her or not.

The taxi driver climbed into the driver's seat and started the cab up.

"An earthquake in New York," he muttered, obviously delighted. "Bet you've never seen that before."

Elsi nodded, craning her neck and watching Mary through the back window. The ghost of a living woman. Mary limped out toward the pond, holding her crippled right hand against her stomach. The taxi pulled out of the parking lot. As they turned the final corner, Elsi glanced at Junior. He was still digging, still crying. He wasn't a ghost. That was how he survived her drugs. He was something else that wanted to be left alone. She respected his wishes and looked away.

Feral

The moon summons me up
from the dust of my father
and the rattling wind of
my mother's voice.

So full tonight so I
can see the way home.
Sunlight has eluded me.
A long time gone. I hurt.

Arthritis hurt, and the deep
ache of flu. It's warm.
That's something. Sometimes
when the hurt comes, I shiver.

My homeward journey is made
by feel, and curious scent.
The way may bleed moonshadows,
but I can smell the imprint of hooves.

The scent is old and the trees
are taller than I remember.
I have been away for three
lifetimes, with the moon for a wife.

The pain deepens now to
bone rattling cramps. My legs
shorten because they have to.
I lie down. It's better lying down.

Jerking and panting in ripple
moonlight, I want this moment to end.
Moments never do. They can be
like lives: long and uncomfortable.

So I run on all fours, tail
behind like my standard.
Nose pointed and ears up.
It's not enough. Pain follows.

Until I'm too animal to think.
Then it stops.

The Quartered Man

I was nine and my cousin was eleven the first time I saw the crossroads. Father had ridden out to the trading camp a few days ahead of us while we waited for more pieces of tinker's ware from my uncle.

About halfway through the three-day ride, Jack brought his horse to a stop. I came up next to him. We were riding through countryside of sparse cottonwood trees, whispering grass, and rolling hills.

"Why'dja stop?" I asked him impatiently. Black birds croaked at us and the winter-bare branches of a nearby tree crackled in the breeze.

"You see that?" He pointed.

There was a crossroads about a hundred yards down the dusty lane. A stone cairn stood where the two roads met.

"The rock pile?"

"Um-hm. And you see that?" He pointed a little to the right.

I squinted and noticed for the first time a detour around the crossroads. A track had been weathered into the dirt. It bowed south just enough to miss the cross, rejoining our road on the far side. It had seen a lot more use than the main cross.

Jack led his horse onto the detour, and I followed.

"Why are we avoiding the crossroads?"

He shrugged. "I don't know. But when you see these detours, you take them."

I was silent for a moment. This was my first long trip outside of the village. Jack had been out dozens of times on trading runs with my father, so he knew things. But this crossroads detour seemed ridiculous. We were passing not ten feet from the crossing and the quiet stone cairn. "It's a pile of rocks," I said.

Jack brought his horse to a stop, and I clamped my mouth shut, fearing I had annoyed him. The sound of black birds replaced the sound of leather and hooves.

"We avoid it because the locals avoid it. They have a reason." He nodded at the cairn. "Most likely someone's buried there."

I felt a chill. "Why would they bury someone in the road?"

Jack leaned toward me and spoke low, like he does when he's trying to scare me. "Sometimes, if someone's been bad, they'll bury 'em head down to send 'em straight to Hell. But sometimes, when a fellah's been really bad, and folks suspect he's got a deal with the Devil, they don't want him going to Hell. He'll just come back up and cause trouble. So they cut him into four pieces and bury him at the four points of a crossroads. Then his ghost'll be too confused to know which way's Heaven and which way's Hell. And he cain't haunt nobody, because he cain't find his way back to town." Jack sat back up and nodded to the cairn. "His head's probably in there."

"And you believe that?" I asked, sneering as best I could, but it sounded weak. My heart beat a little faster when we kicked our horses and moved away from the crossing.

"If the local folks are gonna ruin a perfectly good crossroad," Jack said without turning to look back, "they must've had a reason."

"What happens if I touch it?" I asked, looking back at the cairn that still looked like an innocent heap of rocks.

"Your father told me the ghost is looking for someone to give it directions. If it can grab you and make you tell, it will. Or maybe it'll trick you into pointing out where the village is. Your father says it'll promise you the world too, but don't believe it."

I wanted to laugh, to show my older cousin I wasn't scared, but my throat was dry.

We met up with Father later and had a busy time at the trading camp by the river. I mostly kept my mind off the stone cairn while working, but at night, going to sleep under my blanket, I kept imagining spooks and haunts coming for me out of the long grasses of the hills. A lot of people were about because trader camps never really sleep, and twice I sat up wide-eyed when someone walked by with a horse or a dog. Then Father ordered me to go to sleep and I didn't dare sit up again.

We took a different way home two days later because Father wanted to pass through the villages up north. We still had some tin-ware, and he intended to sell it all. I was disappointed that we didn't see the crossroads again, but not too disappointed.

Jack and I came back through a number of times as the years passed, and we always rode around the crossroads. Then one day, when I was about twenty, I came through alone. Jack was already at the trader camp with his son, and I was joining him with a few more pieces Father had hammered out. Father's leg was bad, so he couldn't come with us anymore, but Jack and I had done this enough times that we haggled as well as he did. This he finally admitted, but he still hadn't allowed that our tin-ware was comparable to his or my uncle's.

I stopped my horse as I came to the top of the hill above the crossroads. The site looked gentler than when I was young. The cottonwoods were swelled large with green and the tall grass and wildflowers rolled with the breeze. The bypass around the crossroads was much more defined now. There were wheel ruts, and the grass had been worn away to twice the width of a cart. The cross itself was a diminishing scar of hardy weeds that had crept out onto the packed dirt. Eventually the prairie would take the crossing back, but not for some years.

I nudged my horse, Addie, down the hill, riding easily. I didn't believe the crossroads was haunted but wanted to prove it to myself. The ever-present blackbirds filled in the silence when I stopped. I swung down and left the horse standing placidly as I walked over the seldom-trodden earth to the cairn.

I wondered if there was a skull in there. Who knew how these rumors started?

Praying quickly, and assuring myself that late morning in the bright sun was the very best time to confront ghosts, I lifted the top rock off the cairn. There was nothing below but the next layer of stones. I set the first rock on the ground, annoyed now at the hollowing whisper of the wind and the calling birds. I removed the next few stones, then the next few. And lifting off a large flat one, I stepped back in mild surprise to see the round, white top of something that certainly wasn't a rock. So there *was* a skull in there.

I pulled away the rock in front of the face to be confronted by a water-stained skull with rotten teeth. Water had collected in tiny puddles in the hollow eye sockets from last week's rains. There were broken vertebrae nestled below the skull. Whoever he was, they had chopped his head off.

Having eased my curiosity, I diligently replaced the stones around the dead man's head. I had set them on the ground in order, so I tried to pile them back in the same way. I set one stone down a little hard on the skull. I picked it up again quickly, but I hadn't broken the bone. As best as I could gauge, the rebuilt cairn looked as it always had, and no one the wiser.

Clapping my hands together to rid my gloves of dust, I turned back to my horse and stopped in surprise.

A middle-aged man stood next to my horse. He was dressed like a farmer, with a bushy beard like the locals wore. The skin of his face and hands was leathery from long hours in the sun, and he had a red bruise on his forehead. He was running his hand along my horse's side, saying softly, "Easy girl. Easy girl." I hadn't heard him come up. How had he walked all the way down the hill without me noticing?

"Mornin'," I said guardedly. It was likely he would take offense at my rock moving. It was equally likely it was his grave I had disturbed. Maybe that knot on his head was from my careless rebuilding.

"Mornin'," he returned amiably.

"I was just curious about this pile of rocks here," I said by way of explanation.

"That's okay," he said, continuing to run his hand along Addie's flank. She didn't seem bothered by him. "There's nothing to the stories anyway."

"That so?"

"Yeah. It's to scare the wee 'uns to make 'em do their chores."

"Somebody's head's in there, so it's not all stories."

"Somebody's head's in there, sure. But no ghost."

"Who's head?"

He shrugged. "I couldn't say. It's been here since afore I was born."

"Really?" I looked back down at the rocks. They sat quietly like they always had; only now I knew what they concealed. I could see the skull in my mind, under the rocks, looking up at me.

"Where you headed?" he asked.

I had been waiting for a question along these lines, and had been trying to think of an answer. If he was a local farmer, it was appropriate for him to want to know my business. But if he was the ghost, he would try to get me to tell him the way home. There was no way of knowing, so I had to be coy. Not that I believe in ghosts, mind you, but it's best to be careful after you've just seen a skull.

"I'm a tinker," I said, pushing enthusiasm into my voice like I wanted to sell him something. I marched forward and pulled out the belt loop that held the pack of pots and pans on Addie's back. With a clash and a rattle, the pots swung down from their strings and hung along my horse's side. "And I'm here to sell to anyone and everyone who has need of a good pot."

He pursed his lips and came around the horse to look at the wares, lifting first one and then another. Looking at the craftsmanship. He still could have been alive or dead, for all I knew.

"Nice work," he said finally. "Yours?"

"My father's."

He nodded. "He does good work, but I don't believe I need any pots just now."

I shrugged and began the loud task of resetting the pots in their bag.

"You heading into town to sell those?"

"I'm headed to the trader's camp. They set it up once a month and I head over when I have something to sell."

"Yeah. Trader's camp. I been there myself once or twice, but not in a while. Not in a couple of years. You been riding long to get here?"

"Not long. A few days. Been taking it easy on this old horse." Trying not to be rude, I swung up onto Addie's back. The farmer didn't seem to mind my elusiveness. He just kept smiling faintly and started walking along beside me as I nudged Addie into motion.

"Treat your animals right," he said, running his hand along her flank again. "They stick by you."

I nodded. This was getting weird. I passed the cairn and moved out onto the outgoing western road.

"You know what time it is?" he asked, stopping about five paces from the cairn.

I kept riding until I was fully on the western road, then stopped and turned to face him. That was a ridiculous question. The sun had passed its peak and was beginning its descent, so it had to be early afternoon. There was no way he couldn't know that, unless he didn't know what direction he was facing and didn't know if the sun was rising or falling. I pondered challenging him. He didn't look like I thought a ghost should look.

"There are some would say you're a ghost," I said finally. His smile didn't fade. "And there are some would say you're not. But I'm not gonna tell you directions or times or where I'm from or where the trader's camp is setting up. If you aren't a ghost, then I'm sorry, but you can't be too careful."

I tried to make it sound apologetic, and he nodded to me once. "You can't be too careful," he said. I started to turn my horse to be on my way, but he wasn't done. "I'd like to see your pots again."

He made no move to advance, so I stopped the horse, facing him at an angle. "You don't need any pots just now, and I haven't got anything else you'd be interested in."

"You could tell me the time."

I grew annoyed. So this was the spirit of the dead man, condemned to stand at the crossroads until someone told him the way home. At least he could be more creative in his requests. My cousin had told me that the ghost would try to trick me into helping him, and failing that, would offer me fabulous trophies. This guy was barely trying. "I haven't got anything else you'd be interested in," I said more forcefully, and turned my horse to go.

"I might have something you'd be interested in," he said, and I stopped once more. I admit I still had no fear of him. He had not done anything to make me afraid.

I tugged Addie around to face him fully, put on my best expression of waiting, and said nothing. He also remained silent. The quiet wind drifted through the grass. A bird croaked in the tree to the north and was answered from another tree down along the road to the south. Crickets hummed.

He inhaled and reached into his pocket. I watched with interest as he pulled out a silver-headed hammer. It was a good hammer. Much nicer than the one I owned. "This is a very special hammer," he said, and I kept waiting, refusing to let out my emotions. "With it you can tap out the most wondrous pots. Better than anything your father ever made, and better than anything you cousin ever will. You'll make a fortune at the trader's camp."

I shrugged. I already knew I was as good as my cousin or my father and had no aspirations for more. And wealth meant little to me. I bought this horse when I was young, and when it died, I'd have enough to buy another. I did enjoy a cup of beer and the ham the town inn served, but I had enough money for those things, too. My clothes I made myself, and I was proud of them.

And besides, there was no telling what a charmed hammer might make. All of my pots might spring leaks, or they might bite their owners. I could be reasonably sure none of my current pots would do that.

He must have felt my indifference, because he slipped the hammer back into his pocket and came up with a rolled parchment and a small cloth sack instead. He lifted the parchment high like it was a torch. I didn't expect much, since I can't read.

"This is a map," he said. "A special map to show you all the beautiful women of the land. And this," he held the cloth sack up, "contains the Powder of Allure. You could find a wife. You could find a dozen wives. You could visit a different woman every night and they would all love you." He grinned a knowing grin.

But again I wasn't all that impressed. I had visited my share of women while traveling the circuit. None of them could rightly be called beautiful, but then I'd never seen what the storytellers call a beautiful woman and figured that was for the best. Men were always getting enchanted by beautiful women in stories, or trying to do courageous things and getting killed. Anni at one of the villages two days' ride north had only one eye and a bad temper, but she wouldn't make you fight a dragon. I was more comfortable with her than I ever would be with a princess.

"No thank you, sir," I said.

Without seeming angry, or dwelling on this second failure, the ghost put the map and powder sack away and pulled out an open-topped sack that jingled with coins. But he pulled it out too quickly and the coins tumbled out before he could catch them. They bounced and rolled and he cursed angrily. A couple of coins reached as far as Addie's hooves and she stepped back nervously, dropping her head to sniff them.

The ghost, all cross now and muttering things to himself that Mother used to box my ears over, bent down to gather the coins and drop them back into the sack. He wasn't too careful, and I saw grass and dirt go in with the money. I just watched him, still not saying anything. If he was clumsy, well then, that was his problem.

But after a little while, when he had gotten up the coins that were piled close to him and he had to start walking around to fetch the ones that had rolled, he stopped and looked up at me. "You know," he said, still mad, "this would go a lot faster if you'd lend me a hand."

I leaned over and looked down at the three small gold circles below me, then sat back up. If I picked up what wasn't mine, then it might become mine under the rules of Finders Keepers, Losers Weepers. And if I accepted a gift from him, then I was beholden to him and maybe he could jump across that circle and grab me and make me tell him which way was town. It was a possibility, and I wasn't taking chances. So I climbed down off the horse and flipped the three coins back to him with my toe.

I mounted Addie again. "I have to be going," I said, tipping my hat cordially.

He straightened from where he was picking up the last of the gold. A forlorn expression came across his face, driving away his angry scowl. "There must be something I could give you for my freedom."

I shrugged. I couldn't think of anything I wanted that was worth releasing him. "I doubt I'm smart enough to come out ahead in the bargain. It's only in the stories where the hero outwits the ghost, so I'll be going."

"You disturbed my sleep." He rubbed at the deepening bruise on his forehead. "You can't leave. We *must* bargain for something."

I tipped my hat to him a second time and headed out of the valley. I looked back when I reached the crest of the hill that would hide the crossroads from my sight. He was still standing there looking up at me. An uneasy feeling wiggled into my belly, and I hurried on to meet with my cousin.

A day later, after a restless sleep in the fields, I rode up the last of the rolling hills that preceded the river. I hadn't smelled wood smoke all morning, but dismissed this as an odd effect of the wind. I hadn't seen any other horsemen or wagons on the hills either, and hoped that I had arrived at a lull in trading. But coming up the last hill, I couldn't hear the dull rumble of hundreds of people and animals or the clank of metal. I grew more and more uneasy until I crested the hill and saw nothing.

There was no camp. The grass was long and untrampled, so no camp had been here in the past few weeks. Why would they have moved? This spot was a day's ride from three large towns and right on the river.

I rode down to the wide river and let my horse drink while I looked over the road that ran along the bank. It was dusty and well used, but there was no arrow pointing to tell me where the camp or my cousin might have gotten to.

I remounted and rode north for several hours to another flat place where they might have gone. Because I hadn't seen another living soul on the way, I knew long before I got there that I would find no camp.

The closest village was another four- or five-hours ride, so I continued on. They should have news of what had happened. If they didn't, I would take the north circuit home and sell my pots. Father would be furious if I came home with everything unsold. My cousin and I usually took the north circuit home because there were more villages. He was probably up there now, taking all my sales. I should reach home three or four days after him.

A few hours later, as the sun dropped, I once more passed cultivated lands. I looked for farmers, and sure enough, I soon saw a man looking down at me from atop a hill.

I waved and turned off the track and rode up to him. He waited without moving, leaning on a rusty old pitchfork with one tine missing. I stopped Addie just out of stabbing range and spread my hands to show they were empty.

"Good afternoon," I said. He nodded to me. There were more fields down in the valley behind him, and a number of people working. This man was their lookout. Perhaps there had been trouble with raiders. Maybe that's why the trader's camp had moved.

"I'm a tinker," I said. It was all the introduction I needed out here. His eyes stayed locked with mine. "I went to the trader's camp a few hours down the river, but there's no one there. Do you know where they moved it to?"

He shook his head faintly. "Hasn't been a trader's camp there for a good long while," he said. "They moved down closer to Brillain when I was a boy."

"The city? But I was at the trader's camp last month."

He shrugged and didn't bother to defend his statement. I stared at him a few moments longer, then started to ride into the valley to ask someone else. He lifted his pitchfork and pointed it at me. "We don't need any pots, tinker," he said without malice. Something bad must have happened to have spooked him.

"Have the farmers had trouble?"

"Not this month, tinker, but you have to be careful."

I nodded and returned to the river road. I could easily have ridden around him, but I sell to a lot of the same people over and over again, and it's best not to get a reputation for causing trouble. Besides, I would reach the village before nightfall. They should be friendlier there. The raiders might attack lone farmsteads, but they had never been numerous enough to bother the towns.

Two hours later, as the sun touched the horizon, I turned east when the road forked away from the river. In minutes I was back in hill country and the river was lost from sight. This whole situation was odd, possibly the oddest thing that had ever happened to me. It had gotten my thoughts all wrapped up and twisted around so that I didn't notice what was in front of me until I was half-way down the hill.

Looking up I yanked my horse to a stop. The crossroads lay in front of me, and the ghost still stood at its edge, smiling faintly. I looked behind me, but there was nothing to see. There were at least ten hills between me and the river.

A little angry, I rode down into the valley, this time taking the branch track that skirted the crossing like I should have the first time. The ghost walked beside me and again stopped at the edge. Glaring at him, I rode on and up the hill. Cresting it, I saw the crossroad in the next valley. The ghost was standing at its edge looking up at me. I turned around and the crossroad was also in the valley behind me. The ghost down there looked up at me. For a moment I was surprised that I couldn't see myself standing on the crest of the next hill.

Resigned, I rode down. "What do you want?" I asked, knowing his answer.

"My freedom, of course," he said. "I offered you skills, women, and money, and you didn't want it. But you woke me up, and now we must bargain. You are trapped here until we do. It seems I finally have something you want."

"There's got to be a way out of this valley. One of these directions."

"Oh, sure," he said. "There's one or two ways out. Maybe you'll find them before you starve to death, but it won't do you any good. Fifty years have passed since you set out. Your family searched for you, and then mourned your death. Your cousin grew old and died, and his children are old now. Everyone you knew is dead."

"Dead? Everyone?" My father and uncle, my cousin and his family? How could they be dead? I had just seen them a few mornings ago. Why had I been so stupid? I only wanted to see what was under the cairn. Why didn't I listen to my father's advice? "How did I get fifty years ahead?"

"Strange things can happen in a crossroads. If you're willing to deal, I can take you back to the moment you left."

"You can?" I instantly knew I had spoken too eagerly. That was a bad way to begin bargaining. I had to think of a plan. I saw that the red lump on his head was gone. "I want more than to just go back."

"Tell me what you want and I'll consider it."

"Let's see." I began to tick off on my fingers. "After you take me back, release me from this valley unharmed. Then don't ever hurt my family, or me, or anyone I know. Don't harm their animals or crops either."

"I can agree to that. Would you like the gold too?"

"No gold. Everything comes from somewhere, and I don't want to know where your gold comes from."

I climbed down off my horse and stepped up to him, standing just a foot away from his face. It struck me as funny, that he looked so normal. They had gone through a lot of trouble to keep this man from coming back, and he looked the same as any other farmer. Probably my cousin was right and he had a contract with the Devil.

"What happens if I break my side of the bargain?" I asked.

"If you lie to me, I am free to do to you as I please. You named your family in the contract, so their fate is on you. I can kill them in a second if you're not careful."

I reached out across the border of the crossroads and he reached back and grasped my hand, though I didn't want to touch him. Now the grin really consumed his face, and I thought a human shouldn't be able to grin that wide or show that many teeth. He let me go and I wiped my palm against my pants.

"Now, tinker," he said, "tell me the way home."

He stepped right to the edge of the crossroads, waiting on me to give him a destination and free him.

"Am I back to the day I met you? The same hour, the same minute?" I circled around to the inside of him, acting like I was afraid and trying to keep my distance.

He looked at me a moment, then said, "Yes."

"And am I free to go?" I took a big step back.

Again he hesitated, then said, "Yes, and I will honor the remainder of our agreement." He stood there waiting, having fulfilled his side of the contract. I didn't doubt he had fulfilled it, and we were back, because they always say in the stories that demons must bow before contracts and obligations.

I took three more steps back, until I was near the cairn. My memory of this place was made complete as the wind whispered across the grass and a black bird called.

Pointing left with my gloved hand, I said, "That's the north road."

Cackling and laughing and howling, the ghost leapt into the air higher than a house. Gray mucous streamers bled from his skin and twirled around him. Addie bolted, but there was nothing to be done about that. I let her go.

Quickly, while he was celebrating, I turned and kicked the cairn as hard as I could. Rocks tumbled. The ghost shrieked and descended, but I already had his skull in my hands. I rapped it sharply against a rock so that it cracked across the back. That old ghost flopped to the ground, screaming and holding his head like a big man who's just lost a bar fight. I was mighty pleased that I had guessed right. I could hurt him. That first bruise on his head had pointed my way.

"We had an agreement." His voice was icy, furious. "Your family will die now because of you."

"I fulfilled it fare and square. Now let's make a new agreement," I said. I ground my finger into the spine hole in the base of his skull. Flecks of bone crumbled off and the ghost doubled over again, howling and thrashing.

I pulled a sack from under my belt and dropped his skull into it. Then I twirled the sack above my head until the ghost staggered back and forth, dizzy.

"That's not fair," he said.

I continued to twirl, keeping him off balance.

"It's not fair," he said again. "I'll trap you here again if you don't release me. Then you'll starve to death and your ghost will haunt this crossroad with me."

"I told you, we need a new agreement." I let the sack fall limp while I fetched Addie. I dragged her back to the edge of the crossroads and remounted. The ghost stood angry and silent the whole while. Suddenly I was consumed by a great itching from feet to head. I couldn't get down fast enough before I fell off, writhing around on the ground trying to scratch away this mind-numbing pain. Then it was gone and I was left gasping for breath, with a newfound appreciation for the damned.

Crawling to my feet, panting, I found that he was at the edge of the circle, feet from me. "I can curse you in so many ways that you'll kill yourself in an hour. Now tell me the way home or your cousin dies! That is the only new bargain I will make."

My heart was pounding and my skin blistered as I yanked his skull from the sack. His lower jawbone fell off as I struggled to get the skull free. The blistering stopped the moment I broke an upper molar off with my thumb. He howled and clutched his mouth. I broke another tooth off. Then a third.

I let him recover, all the while holding the skull out in front of me with my thumb pressed against a fourth tooth. He was trembling, and I could finally see fear in his eyes. As I had hoped, he was a coward. Even with all his power, he was a coward.

I drew my tinker's hammer from my belt. "I need a better bargain, or I start using my hammer."

"It's not fair," he said again.

"For this new bargain, I want everything you promised me last time. In return, you get your skull back."

"No! Tell me the way home."

I tapped his cheekbone expertly with my hammer and a tiny flake chipped off.

"No, no, no!" he howled around broken teeth and a rapidly swelling cheek. "I promise. I promise everything."

So we shook hands much like the first time, only less cordial. I fulfilled my end of the new bargain by tossing him his skull. "I'd bury that in the cairn if I was you. It's not safe out here."

"I will kill you," he muttered as he began stacking rocks. "Somehow. You broke our bargain."

"I did not. And you didn't make such a good deal in the second bargain." I pulled his lower jaw from my sack. "You only bargained to get your skull back. If I ever feel so much as an ounce of pain from you, or if one of my friends or family comes down with a curse, then I'm starting in on your jawbone. I can make it last a long time if I only take off tiny bits." I waved the hammer back and forth. "You remember that."

And there I left him, standing angry and afraid and damned. This time I didn't look back as I rode away. I headed west to the trader's camp and my cousin. And I did end up with a boon after all. It turns out the jawbone can talk, and doesn't like the old ghost very much. It tells me all kinds of wonderful stories, and I feed it sweets.

Immortal Evelyn

Nothing lasts forever, Evelyn thought in angry frustration, *except me*. She had seen her capitol built, and now she watched it fall.

The smell of blood tainted the smoke as she pulled Jonathan, her only surviving Hammer, down a half-collapsed corridor. Her path was lit by the fires shining through broken windows.

Her body shook from exhaustion, from magical depletion and the voracious magics she'd wrought, from burnt adrenalin, from death. She hated feeling so out of control. Princess Angrassa was destroying everything Evelyn had built over the last five hundred years.

"They're close," Jonathan wheezed, staring back down the corridor where they could hear shouting. Evelyn checked his throat where she'd tried to seal a deep, bloody gash. His brown hair was ash-filthy and slicked back with sweat.

"We'll make it." Evelyn kept her voice firm.

They retraced their steps down passageways that had changed hands a dozen times in the last two hours, stumbling over bodies. Evelyn didn't look at faces, but she knew who they were. She was furious with herself. How had she been taken by surprise? The entire Senate, their mightiest wizards, had gone down to depletion. You could see it on the royalist side too, when the Princess's wizards would suddenly stumble or fail to raise a shield in the face of a cleaving spell.

The greatest carnage began after the Hammers' engagement. Hammers were not true wizards, but they possessed savage strength. Princess Angrassa and her powerful husband, Thurious, had developed more of them in exile than anyone could have predicted, and they were attacking the *Senate* at its heart.

For nearly five hundred years Evelyn had guided the kings and queens of the rising empire and had died twice defending them. Then fifteen years ago she'd ended the royal line with a grieving heart. She created the Senate rather than allow Princess Angrassa to take the throne.

"Careful." Evelyn helped Jonathan over rubble by a gaping hole in the wall. She felt a cool breeze and caught sight of evening stars. In the distance, fighting raged for the castle's western wing and flames crept up the ivy of the battlements. Glancing down, Evelyn noted bodies in the courtyard, clustered near a blocked gate. It was all a waste.

She kicked her blackened, yellow dress from a snag, irritated. She needed something practical to wear.

"Just ahead," she encouraged. "There's a way out."

She led him through a once-grand door, gone now, brass hinges hanging twisted from the frame. How close was their pursuit? She'd already brought down scores of royalist wizards and Hammers tonight, reminding them of why she was a legend, but she didn't want to die again. Death stole her memory.

She pulled Jonathan into the observatory. It tore Evelyn's heart to see the wreckage. Above them, the great Orrery of the Ages towered, with mechanical planets and moons on tracks around a brass sun. It should have been gliding silently on its rotational course as it had for three hundred years, but now several massive bronze armatures had been twisted over and planets lay crushed on the flagstones. A hole the size of a donkey had been punched through the sun, shattering the glass-domed ceiling above it. And all around, bodies in green or red lay under a layer of freshly fallen glass.

Evelyn suddenly remembered playing beneath the Orrery as a child, a memory as clear as day. It couldn't be real, though, and she rejected it. She'd been alive for two hundred years before the machine was built, the histories said so. Her memories of things prior to her last death were etched and scored, based on history books rather than actual recollection, but this was one of the impossible memories that cropped up from time to time. It was probably a hallucination brought on by her current depletion.

She helped Jonathan to the great, geared axis that supported the planets. It had once turned as she turned, implacable. Now the gears were motionless and there was an acrid stench of burnt metal and oil. "Up you go." She pointed at the axle. Smaller gears could act as steps. "Get onto the roof and find Senator Kouler."

Jonathan grabbed her hands. "You're not coming?"

Evelyn squeezed his fingers back. "I'm going after Princess Angrassa," she said. "I'm the only one left who can."

His expression was riven. "I tried as hard as I could."

Evelyn had never paid much attention to him because he was just a Hammer, but now she took his face in her hands and looked into his eyes. "You survived when many others didn't, and you stayed when many others ran. I'm proud of you."

"Evelyn Aeterna!"

Evelyn smiled. "Go help Senator Kouler. I'll still be here standing after this is done."

Tears shimmered on his lashes as he began to climb. He kept looking back until he reached the top and scrambled out of sight.

Evelyn hoped he'd make it. She'd grown to like him.

She spun and walked deeper into the observatory, her magical depletion yawning like a hungry gulf in her stomach. It had been centuries since she'd drained her reserves so low.

She couldn't believe it had come to this. Princess Angrassa had been a brilliant apprentice, destined to be a mighty queen. She'd been warm and funny and so intelligent. Her magic was effortless. Then she met foreign-born Thurious. Evelyn had loathed him from the first, and few people could rouse strong emotions in her anymore. Angrassa's magic and ambitions turned dark so quickly that Evelyn had been forced to intercede.

She heard shouting, the Hammers drawing close, so she hurried through the Gear Master's quarters and slipped out into narrow, back-corridors.

Emerging at the library, she found her way blocked by a raging fire. Anger flared as she stared into the roaring stacks. So many irreplaceable books. Wizards, indistinct through the heavy smoke, fought the flames but the room was lost. There would be so much rebuilding to do.

Evelyn took a deep breath and held it, then charged into the smoke. Her skin prickled from heat and her eyes teared as she ran up an iron, spiral staircase that radiated heat. She burst through the king's doors at last and shoved them closed with blistered hands, gasping a deep breath. She doubled over coughing. Her yellow sleeves hung filthy with ash, and she had to stamp out embers on her hem.

Where was she? The room had been converted to storage at some point. The royal wing had stood abandoned for the last fifteen years, but still she knew it well.

Forcing herself between piles of furniture, yanking her skirts after her, she strode through empty sitting rooms and unlit corridors until she reached the throne-room doors. There was magic nearby. For the first time in memory, she hesitated.

Did she have the strength for this fight? Would it be smarter to escape and wait for another day?

She scolded herself for being a coward. What she really feared was dying again. The Dilernum Siege was her last death, one hundred and forty years ago, at the hands of the mighty wizard Russef. She'd brought herself back and killed him in her post-resurrection delirium, but she'd never recovered her memory.

She looked through nearby windows. The main mass of the castle had gone dark in parts and was crowned with leaping flames in others. Her resolve firmed. She had to end this. The surviving senators and the people of the city depended on her, and death was no excuse.

Marshalling what strength she had, she barged through the throne room doors before they could prepare. A score of people wearing red snapped around to face her and a puncture-spell whipped at her. She blocked it hard and knifed her own spell back, toppling an overeager Hammer at the edge of the Princess' crowd. She threw another attack, and then stopped, feeling the bite of depletion. She had to be very careful.

The Hammers had stumbled back at her attack, but they regrouped nervously in front of the princess on the dais. Around the room, hundreds of fat candles flickered on the floor. Stained-glass windows shimmered.

Evelyn met the eyes of the princess for the first time in fifteen years and saw determination and fear. She wore white and perched on a chair that was likely borrowed from the dining gallery. She had aged and her olive skin had darkened, but Evelyn still pictured the little girl she'd once taught magic to in the gardens. Angrassa's black tresses were chopped to her shoulders.

Evelyn's anger rose like an ascending bird, and she tamped it back down before speaking.

"You came to the throne room before the battle was won," she said softly. "That's presumptuous."

Four Hammers edged shifted on the dais.

"Evelyn Aeterna," Princess Angrassa blurted in a high voice that came out too loud. "Evelyn Immortalis. Evelyn the Everlasting."

"I've missed you, Princess," Evelyn said.

"I am *Queen*," Angrassa replied tightly. "Have you come alone?"

"Has there ever needed to be more than one of me? That's not a throne."

Princess Angrassa blushed. "Where's the real throne?"

"I burned it. We burned everything."

The princess' blush turned white as she clenched her jaw.

"It doesn't matter what she sits on," barked the deep, accented voice of her husband. He stepped forward and Evelyn tore her eyes away from Angrassa to look at him. He'd grown a thick, brown beard, and his pale skin looked stark in the candlelight. He was more dangerous than the Hammers, and Evelyn had never been able to stand him. "A chair, a throne, it doesn't matter," he continued. "The monarchy is restored."

"Thurious," Evelyn said, gathering thin reserves of magic, preparing shields. "You're looking well." In fact, he was. Fifteen years gone and he was still as stout and handsome as he had been before the exile.

"And you don't look a day older."

"Hair dye." She looked back to the princess. "I'm not really immortal, you know. Time toys with me just as it does with everyone."

"Not immortal?" Angrassa said. "Every schoolchild is taught that you were killed twice and brought yourself back."

"That is so." Evelyn didn't remember, but she could recite the histories well enough. "I was stabbed by the priests of the temple and was reborn stronger; I was burned by the wizard Russef and was reborn stronger. What now? You can't hold this city — you lost too many people taking it."

"The Senate is done!" Thurious stated flatly.

"What now?" Evelyn repeated to Angrassa, holding eye contact. "Will you try to kill me a third time, knowing the risks?"

The princess's nostrils flared, then she said simply, "Yes."

"It doesn't have to be this way. Princess! Angrassa. Come back to me."

Angrassa laughed and it sounded bitter and dead. "No."

Her four Hammers threw unfocused, destructive spells, as was their sole ability. Prepared, Evelyn instantly raised shields and braced herself. The joint concussive blast sheared apart and crashed into the wall behind her as she was driven back a step. The Hammers' eyes grew wide, but Thurious' eyes seemed calculating. Evelyn knew he suspected that she couldn't take another hit like that.

So she circled, searching for an angle of attack that would let her go on the offensive. "You have a plan, don't you? Something you're proud of."

The crowd on the dais turned to follow her. Evelyn kept an eye on the Hammers, but she knew the assault would ultimately come from Thurious or Angrassa. Despite her dislike, she respected Thurious immensely. They called him The Wolf.

One of the Hammers made a move and Evelyn threw a strike that ripped through his shields and his heart. He dropped hard while the crowd on the dais panicked. This time they left Angrassa exposed. Evelyn instantly hurled a caustic spell that ricocheted off the stained-glass windows, melting lead, and rebounded at their backs. Thurious barely raised shields over Angrassa while two acolytes fell screaming, legs liquefying.

Angrassa looking shocked and her crowd broke for the door.

"Reveal your plan," Evelyn called over the hoarse screaming, readying her failing reserves for their counterattack.

Princess Angrassa stood awkwardly on a shortened leg, a remnant of a childhood riding accident. She flared her hands and the spell that instantly swarmed out of her fingertips like angry bees was both profoundly powerful and subtly complex. Even as Evelyn raised thick shields, she was delighted by the spiraling inversions in the attack. If Thurious hadn't lured her away, Evelyn knew she could have made Angrassa a great queen.

She whipped a killing strike around the edge of the oncoming swarm, saddened at all the centuries of knowledge and friendships she was about to lose when she died.

Then the shock front of Angrassa's spell hit her hard and chewed into her shields while Evelyn fought. The body of the spell broke through, shredding her clothing and skin. Everything within her was torn.

Evelyn felt vertigo as she dropped through a shimmering wash of colors. She was insubstantial and struggled to hold onto thought. Was she dead? Pain radiated across her skin and helped anchor her.

What had Angrassa done? That spell didn't spring from any of Evelyn's teachings.

The colors abruptly peeled back, and she fell hard onto freezing flagstones. Shocked, she tried to scramble to her feet, but her legs wouldn't cooperate. She fell again, then sat panting, chest heaving, in the center of a large, stone room. She felt slow-witted and sought to find her bearings.

The throne room! It was empty, with no wooden chair on the dais. The royalists had fled. Then it dawned on her that she still had her memory. Her heart lifted. To keep her memory was to keep herself, unbroken. But why?

She stood again, like a new-born colt with unsure steps, shivering. The stained-glass windows were gone, and their gaping wooden frames were charred. A breeze cut through Evelyn's thin, summer gown. Outside, the sky was gray-blue and distant.

She limped painfully to the nearest window and leaned on the frame, taking in the desolation. The castle's western wing was a crumbled husk. Its roof had collapsed, exposing charred rafters. To her left, the Tower of Penance had fallen into a heap of stone. She couldn't see the library wing or her own tower. Desiccated tangles of grass and leafless saplings spread wild across what had been manicured lawns. Time had passed and it was winter.

Not everything was abandoned, she noted. Smoke rose from several chimneys.

Her eyes caught movement amidst the overgrown weeds. Someone was walking on a path. A woman, hands crossed over her chest, walking unsteadily with her head down. She wore a bright, yellow dress like Evelyn's.

There was a thump behind her, and Evelyn spun to find a copy of herself sitting dazed amidst a heap of yellow skirts. "What?" She stared as her shivering twin looked around. When their eyes met, her twin gasped and tried to leap to her feet. She fell as Evelyn had fallen.

"Give it time," Evelyn said.

"Angrassa fragmented me," her twin said.

"Temporal fragmenting." Understanding dawned on her. "Several seasons have gone by." She gestured weakly at the windows.

"That was quite a spell," her twin said, grinning.

"There's another one of us out on the grounds, there."

"I expect a bunch of us will start emerging soon. How many, though?" Her twin stood slowly, tottering. "I'm faint."

"We only have the strength of our fragmented parts." Evelyn snapped her fingers, and nothing happened. "Very little magic," she grunted, upset. "Not enough of me in this body to support it." She felt exposed without magic. She felt beaten. She couldn't be beaten, she was Evelyn Aeterna, protector of the empire. She *was* the empire.

Her twin burst into laughter, holding herself, rocking back and forth. "Where did they come up with a spell like that?" she said with delight. "I'm impressed. They found a way around our power by shattering us."

Evelyn grew irritated by her twin's reaction. "Stop laughing," she snapped.

But her twin didn't stop. "Come on, you have to admit it's clever," she said, wiping her eyes with the heel of her hand. "I clearly got silliness in the splintering. You must have gotten anger."

"Forcefulness and sensibility," Evelyn said, "not anger." If her twin was right, then the splintering had to be extensive for their remnant bodies to lack a full range of emotions. "Wait! I can feel you. And I can feel *her* down on the grounds."

Her twin gasped. "I can too, but I don't feel anyone else."

Evelyn stretched out her arms, sensing the other two twins. Both felt like odd phantom limbs. "So we *are* the first."

"Unless Thurious killed any others who appeared before."

"What a terrible thought." Evelyn wondered if a fragment would ever truly die. She was not used to feeling vulnerable and didn't like it. "Let's get the one outside. We need to reunite with whatever we've got so we can defend ourselves."

Her twin walked unsteadily to the windows and scanned the ruins. One of her legs seemed twisted. "Something went wrong," she mused. "Angrassa wouldn't have abandoned the seat of her ancestors."

"Maybe Senator Kouler regrouped and fought back; he always was one hell of a tactician. I, we, warned her. She should have negotiated."

"She wouldn't have. She'd assume she'd won after I died."

"After we get our fragment from below, let's find out who's tending those fireplaces." Evelyn pointed to the smoke drifting up from the stacks. "I'm freezing."

"Oh! Did you feel that?"

Evelyn closed her eyes. A fourth Evelyn had appeared about a mile west, in a stream. She was soaking wet and frightened.

"Let's get her before she catches pneumonia."

And thus began the gathering of Evelyns that resulted in nine by evening. The original Evelyn quickly found she didn't have patience for her emotionally fraught twins. There were two sullen ones who cried; the chipper one from the throne room who bounced about and laughed; a curious one; a hateful one who didn't want to help; a revolted one who didn't want to touch anything and kept washing her hands in pools of freezing water; an anxious one who stared with wide eyes; and another forceful one who contradicted everyone.

They also discovered that the central wing of the castle was still inhabited by the ancient and dutiful families who had always lived there, even though the castle was half ruined and marooned on disputed land. The bustling capitol outside the castle walls was abandoned.

"It's been terrible," Andrus the Steward told them in the warm kitchen where soup was generously provided from thin winter stores. Evelyn had known him since he was a child. "King Thurious battles First Senator Kouler. Their armies trample the land and take food while the people starve. A lot of folks headed south last winter and never came back."

A score of thin men and women had gathered behind Andrus, staring from one Evelyn to the next in open wonder.

"Where's Princess Angrassa?" one of the Sad Evelyn's asked.

Andrus looked down. "Naught been seen of her since you vanished. King Thurious claimed the kingship."

Evelyn perched on the edge of a table and stared at the aspects of herself. Did she really look like that? Her hair was a wreck after the long night of fighting, yanked up in an off-center bun that she self-consciously fixed on her own head. Her dress was singed and filthy and torn, yellow only because it was bright enough to outshine the abuse it had taken. One of her eyes drooped, her nose was crooked, and her mouth frowned too much. Why did she stand like that, stoop shouldered and awkward? She grew self-conscious and saw others staring at themselves too. She was behaving like a young woman with a mirror, but she couldn't help it.

"Have you returned to end this, Evelyn Aeterna?" said an old woman wearing a threadbare but carefully laundered apron. Her gaze was reverent, worshipful, and she looked at each Evelyn in turn with desperate hope. "Will you put things right?"

"We will," Evelyn said with certainty. She turned to her twins. "We need to unite."

"I agree," said her forceful twin. "I've worked out how Angrassa fragmented us."

"Me too," Evelyn said. "Everything but the temporal part. That must have come on the last wave of the spell."

"Then we can reverse what she did and unite."

"Wait," Anxious Evelyn said, backing up. "I don't want to unite. It might not work. I could die."

"You're not dying. You're rejoining me."

"What do you mean joining you," Evelyn demanded. "They should join me. I was the first. I'm the primary."

"Primary?! We're all equal parts."

"You should join *me*," said Anxious Evelyn. "Come into my body."

"There's no 'body'," Forceful Evelyn retorted. "We're all *the body*."

"Then join me," Evelyn said. Somehow, joining felt like dying. Logically she was just reuniting herself, but deep inside she was terrified of submitting.

"No, join me," said both Sad Evelyns.

"Don't touch me," said Revolted Evelyn. "Nobody touch me. You're all filthy. We need a bath."

"Can't we all join at once?" said Happy Evelyn. She clapped her hands together as if to demonstrate that they could simply run at each other in the middle of the crowded room.

"The spell won't work that way," Evelyn and her forceful twin both said at once.

The castle staff looked on nervously and several maids edged back. The fire crackled warmly.

"What do we do?" Anxious Evelyn said.

"We stop wasting time," Forceful Evelyn said. She grabbed Anxious by the front of her dress, fingers already grinding through the reverse spell, and pulled her into herself with a jerk. Anxious vanished.

Forceful snatched up Happy and Revolted as the rest of the Evelyns scrambled away. The castle staff fled.

"What are you doing?" Evelyn shouted as the remaining four fragments clustered behind her.

"Doing what needs to be done," Forceful Evelyn stated calmly. "It's what I've always done, isn't it? Act quickly and grieve later? It's why there are more decisive and sad variants of me than any other. Now come here. I'm four, let's be nine."

Evelyn felt a stab of dislike. She never submitted to anyone, including herself, and she never gave up. She didn't feel that this was a character flaw.

"Listen," she said softly, turning to the four behind her. They leaned close and in one, swift motion she absorbed them all.

"Stop!" shouted her twin.

Evelyn turned to face her. "I am five." Emotions warred inside her. She'd gotten both sads, the curious, and the hateful one. Now she felt angry and paranoid. Why weren't the personalities integrating? "Let's be nine."

"They were coming to me!"

"No, they weren't."

They both raised hands and began spells, but little magic emerged. Evelyn grew frustrated. How extensively had Angrassa shattered her?

She dropped her hands back to her sides. "We should unite," she said in what she hoped was a reasonable tone. "Merge, not absorb. We'll be stronger." She thrust out her hand.

Her twin hesitated and then took it, and Evelyn briefly marveled at how odd it felt to hold her own hand. There was no time to dwell on it, though, because her twin began the finger movements to absorb her.

"Not nice," Evelyn snarled, yanking her arm even as her finger movements countered her twin's spells. They were too evenly matched, and their clasped hands did not transfer into a merge or an absorption.

They broke off and staggered back, glaring from across the kitchen.

"So what do we do?" her twin demanded.

"We have to unite," Evelyn said, disliking her twin with an intensity that was growing. Her twin's bun had partially come out and tangles of hair hung down her back. She looked ridiculous. "This is ridiculous."

"I agree, but I don't want to give in. I can't."

"Me either," Evelyn said, surprised out of her momentary critical review. "I'm not like this. I'm practical."

"Thurious and Angrassa did something."

"Damn it!" She was right. This overwhelming paranoia, this desire to overcome her twins, this incomplete absorption. "They put something in it to keep us from reuniting."

Like a bell ringing, Evelyn suddenly felt a tenth fragment appear. Not far, maybe half a mile away, outside the stable gates. The fragment was confused and disoriented. From the look on her twin's face, she'd felt it too.

Evelyn was overcome by a burning need to get to that new fragment first. That was how they would all reunite! Evelyn would absorb enough fragments to regain her magic, and then she would drag this lesser twin into herself, kicking and screaming.

They both started running, crashing into each other at the door to the kitchens, scratching and clawing. Then Evelyn's head was cracked back from a tremendous blow, and she stumbled. The world swam. Her twin stood over her, clutching a skillet.

Forceful immediately attempted to absorb her, but Evelyn shielded herself.

"Fine, do it the hard way," her twin said, throwing away the skillet and hurrying down the corridor.

Evelyn sat up, groaning, pressing the heel of her hand to her bleeding cheek. Now that her twin had gone, she regained control. Thurious and Angrassa *must* have poisoned the fragmentation. It was genius. Frustrating genius.

Angrassa shouldn't have had the skills for this.

Evelyn cocked her head, listening, as an eleventh fragment appeared to the south. A few miles this time. The scattering of the fragments was getting wider, spreading out like ripples.

And just like that, reason fled. She scrambled to her feet, driven by a burning desire to reach this fragment while her twin was chasing down the tenth. It was the only way to survive.

A new fragment of Evelyn soared through contrasting, clashing colors. She felt nauseous and everything hurt, and she struggled to hold her thoughts together. Angrassa's spell had done something unexpected.

Her thoughts circled back upon themselves over and over as if they were new, though she was sure she'd thought them before. Time passed.

The colors began to fade while the feeling of weight increased. Finally she dropped hard onto old leaves and lay stunned, looking up through a high tree-canopy at dappled sunshine. Where was she?

She sat up slowly as a bone-deep ache spread throughout her body. Dazed, she smoothed out the burned fabric of her yellow dress.

She froze at a noise. Someone was pushing through a thicket of Mountain Laurel. She heard a curse. A woman's voice. The woman fought clear of the snags and emerged wearing a yellow dress like Evelyn's, though filthy and tattered. The woman's hair was matted.

They stared at each other, and Evelyn was dumbfounded to recognize herself. Were those wild eyes hers?

"I've been fragmented?" she said.

"Temporal fragmentation," the other Evelyn rasped. "Weeks ago."

"What happened to you?"

"Angrassa's spell. We're hunting her to make her fix it."

"How many of us are there?" Why was this other self so feral?

The woman approached and held out her hand. "There are only two. We're attacking King Thurious' army."

Evelyn tried to rise, but her legs were unsteady. "Well there are three of us now."

"No, only two."

As their hands met, Evelyn felt herself pulled into this other. She struggled, but in moments she joined a chorus of other voices, looking out through familiar eyes.

Evelyn sat naked on a warm rock by a waterfall, staring into the rippling, hurrying current. Her yellow dress, dirty and kissed by fire, lay folded beside her. She was bruised from her fall, and weak, but in a pleasant mood. All of this meant something, she was sure—the flying through colors, the bump on the ground, even this waterfall—if only she could collect her thoughts.

She trusted that something wonderful would happen next. Angrassa had banished her, but all banishments could be circumvented.

The trees tossed joyfully in the wind and leaves, brilliant orange and red, fluttered to the ground. She wondered if she should jump into the stream. Would that clear her head? She just had to overcome her sleepy languor and climb into the water. Cold water. Delicious.

"Oh, hello," she said, smiling as someone carefully climbed down the embankment nearby. Someone who looked very much like her, though she wore royal red and had a ragged scar across one cheek. The woman's hair was long and braided. "Are you me?"

"I'm many of us," the woman said in a weary voice.

"Oh," Evelyn said, returning to her contemplation of the river.

"Don't you want to know what's going on?"

"You can tell me," Evelyn said, "or we can swim."

"You're one of the happy ones, aren't you?"

"Content."

"There are never a lot of you. Never enough. I like you."

Evelyn smiled. "I like you too."

The stranger held out her hand and Evelyn took it. As she became one with the woman in red, she sensed great pain and hunger. She wanted to soothe that gaping wound, but it was very wide and deep.

Evelyn fell through light and color, struggling. She'd been in a daze, but now her thoughts grew clear.

Princess Angrassa had killed her! The worst part of dying would be the forgetting, and she dreaded awakening. She didn't want to start all over.

The colors vanished and Evelyn dropped hard onto warm dirt, knocking the breath out of her. Sunshine was blinding. She tried to scramble to her feet but toppled back. Why was she outdoors?

Then she realized she could remember! Her thoughts were her own!

She caught sight of a white, split-rail fence and startled goats staring at her before a sack was yanked over her head.

She fought, cursing and scratching, but felt agonizingly weak. Where was her magic, damn it? They bound her arms and ankles and hefted her onto a rough, wooden surface. A horse whinnied and the cart began to bump forward. There were voices. She was in the midst of many people on the move.

"Let me go!" she shouted, trying to move her fingers behind her back. Still no magic. She yanked her hands against the ropes, feeling nauseous. What had Princess Angrassa done?

"Settle down," ordered a man's voice nearby.

She fought harder. "Who's there?"

"Don't say anything," barked another man nearer the horse.

She had to get out of here! She needed to see. She struggled, wrenching her shoulder and whacking her head against the side-rails of the cart.

"Great," the first man said. "She's one of the skittish ones. It's gonna be a long ride."

"What do you mean?" Evelyn demanded. "Do you know who I am?" She wasn't skittish, she was exhausted and starving and in pain. She'd fought a terrible battle.

"We know who you are. Relax. We got a ride of a couple hours."

So she settled back, listening, but the two men never spoke again. Evelyn was left with the squeak of the wheels, the clop of hooves, and the rising and falling rumble of voices in the crowd. She breathed the rough fibers of the sack and yanked the ropes until her hands were swollen and numb. Her magic wasn't entirely gone, she could feel the barest edge of it. If she could grab hold of it, she could fight.

Once she kicked out hard and hit the man in some meaty part of his body, and he grunted and moved quickly across the cart.

"Dammit," he muttered. "I hate when you do that. You'd think I'd learn."

"What does that mean?" she demanded.

He didn't reply.

Hours passed. Evelyn grew increasingly uncomfortable on the hard boards in the hot sun. She was listening in a half-daze to what felt like echoes of her own thoughts, two sets of thoughts, approaching from the east. They were chaotic and urgent.

Her cart suddenly entered into shade and circled to a stop while the larger group continued on around them. The near man shoved himself off the back of the cart.

"Wow, I've tightened up," he said, his boots scuffing ground. "The years are unkind, eh?"

"Get her inside before the others get here," the older man said, and Evelyn was hoisted by the armpits and ankles. Again she struggled, but there was no energy in her.

Apparently 'inside' was a bit of a walk, because it took some climbing up a hill before the sounds around her abruptly changed to hollow silence, broken by their breathing and boots scraping. The air was chill, and she grew more alert. The churning thoughts of the two other Evelyns vanished.

She was set down roughly next to a fire that glowed ruddy through the sack. When the sack was finally lifted off, she spat. She lay in a cave, a good distance from the bright cave opening, with complex sigils chiseled into the walls. Men in red uniforms stood about.

Someone placed an ornate chair on the opposite side of the fire and a man in a red cloak limped into view.

"Thurious?" she said, stunned to see a much older version stiffly lowering himself to the chair. He was paler than ever, and his leg jutted out from an injury.

"Evelyn Aeterna," Thurious rumbled. His accent had faded. "The great thorn in my side."

"Where am I? Time has passed, hasn't it?" His hair had gone gray and thin, and his once handsome face had grown lined behind a beard. One eye looked cloudy.

"Yes, time has passed. Twenty years, give or take."

"Why am I so weak?" She pulled against her restraints.

A man with a sharply angled face stepped up to her left, fingering a knife-hilt at his belt.

"Queen Angrassa's spell fragmented you in space and time. You've been reappearing for twenty years, and two versions of yourself have snatched up most of the fragments. They're searching for you now."

Those must be the other thoughts she'd sensed. "You've kidnapped me before, haven't you?" she said, eyeing the disquieting man with the knife.

"Of course," Thurious stated flatly, "because I need your help. The two greater Evelyns have grown to fifty or more fragments apiece, and they're at war."

"What?" Evelyn gasped.

"They're destroying everything."

"Why?"

"They're insane. Each fragment is too out of synchronicity to reunite, but they've forced union. It's driven them mad. I never expected you'd try to do it."

"I am eternal."

"You are annoying!"

Evelyn frowned. "So the fragments, we, are emerging at different times and different harmonics." she said, her mind racing. "We can align them, though."

"I'm not aligning you just to have you take control again. This is *my* kingdom!"

"This is a cave."

He reared up, fists clenched. "The crown is mine," he snapped. "What's left of your Senate is cowering down at Gurith."

Evelyn flinched, then grew upset at her own flinch. The young man had called her one of the skittish ones, hadn't he? "Where's Princess Angrassa?"

"Dead. Pleasantries aside, tell me what you know about your immortality," he said, easing back in his seat. "There are no myths of your creation. Nothing of your birth or childhood or ascension to inform me how to unmake you, you just appeared out of the mists! Even your smallest fragments are ageless."

"I won't help you," she said, sad to hear of Angrassa's death.

"Your two greater selves must be stopped."

"I can't be killed," she said firmly. "I come back stronger after I die."

"No. I've laid several of you open wide and you didn't come back. You are killable."

Her throat tightened. "You killed my other fragments?"

He shifted his stiff leg. "Mostly. I poisoned some and released them to be absorbed by your other selves."

"Poison?"

"I added temporal noise. Harmonic resonance."

"What? That would..."

"Make the fragments more asynchronous, I know, but it didn't kill your other selves as I'd hoped. It unfortunately drove them further insane."

"Where did you learn temporal magic?" she demanded, dumbfounded.

"Here and there. I've grown adept."

She doubted he understood the theory at all. "You can't twist time, resonant or not. It's uncontrollable. It feeds back on itself, trying to smooth out the discontinuities."

"And yet here I sit and there you sit," he said, unsmiling. "Tell me how to kill you."

"What you've done to those two Evelyns is abhorrent," she snapped. "I won't help you."

He chewed on his cheek, then looked away. "They must be dealt with. These are the burdens of a king."

"If the other fragments couldn't tell you what you want, why do you keep grabbing us up?"

"Different fragments remember different things. It would be fascinating if it weren't so tedious having to do this over and over. What do you remember of your origins?"

Evelyn shook her head. "I only remember my current incarnation."

"You remember more than you think."

Evelyn's heart beat harder in her chest, but she kept her voice steady. She'd escaped worse. "There's nothing in my old journals about my childhood."

"I read them." He leaned forward and made the fingers of his right hand dance a complex dance. "What have you forgotten?"

The memory Thurious pried free was exceptionally odd, and Evelyn knew it was false. She was an aging queen. She sat at her dressing table, hair pinned up, while servants applied concealers and moisturizers to erase the marks of time. She felt tired. She'd never felt so old or stiff in her life.

"No!" came Thurious' voice, bursting into her dream. "This memory is not yours. Again."

Another broken memory floated up of a fierce battle. She rode a horse and wore armor. She was a man, a commander, urgently racing to the front to bolster a failing line.

"Again."

Thurious forced four more untethered memories up from her mind before giving up. Evelyn raised her shaking head. He glared at her with one piercing, blue eye.

"You are the most infuriating thing, you know that? You're not even all that powerful, you're just unkillable. Like a cockroach."

He turned suddenly and looked down the tunnel to the cave entrance. "One of them's coming." He nodded to the man standing to the side, who immediately drew his knife.

"Your liver's actually the most important part of this useless exercise," Thurious said, climbing to his feet. "I've learned some great and holy truths scrying the intricacies of your liver. It's fascinating. And your heart... your heart beats with the power of immortality. It *will* tell me why."

Evelyn jerked her bonds desperately. She found flame magic at last and lit them.

"Don't worry," the knife-man said, patting out the flames. "Your belly to your breastbone goes quick. The breastbone, though, takes work."

Evelyn lay bound with a sack over her head, but she didn't struggle or speak. Amidst the jangle of harness bells and creak of leather, the clop of hooves and groaning of the cart where she lay, she counted at least twenty voices. They'd been waiting for her.

Her body was wracked with the aftereffects of the spell, but her mind was clear. Her death at Princess Angrassa's hands was vivid. Why could she remember this time? And why had her magic gone?

So Evelyn listened to the voices and call of blackbirds and thrum of crickets. She began to sense a world far removed. The feeling grew, and she soon heard three echoes of herself.

The eldest two Evelyns were south of her by some miles, battling with vicious, feral magic. There was poison in their bodies and minds, and a frantic nature to their power. Their loss of control frightened her.

She guessed that she'd been fragmented, and that some portion of her fragments had tried to unify. It had gone badly wrong.

The third embodiment, the youngest by far, was to the north, heading this way at a great rate of speed. She seemed focused and lucid.

Evelyn yearned to become part of them with an almost painful need. It wasn't unexpected, given her fragmentation, and she fought the feeling. She needed to keep her head clear.

How had Angrassa and Thurious shattered her? How many pieces, and how far had she been strewn?

She strained to sense the river of time, which swept by her on all sides. She easily found several dozen fragments of herself still there in the time-current, oblivious. So there was a temporal part to her fragmentation.

The cart stopped and hands hoisted her up.

Again she didn't struggle as they carried her but listened to her other three selves racing to reach her. The lucid Evelyn should arrive first; she was moving very fast.

They entered the hush of pine woods, and she heard the muffled press of feet on a carpet of needles. Another few minutes and there came the sound of hacking at bushes. She was carried forward through briars that tugged and clawed at her, then she returned to sunlight.

The connection to her other three selves was severed so abruptly she gasped. She'd been blocked.

Evelyn was lowered into deep grass. As she pushed herself up with her bound hands, the sack was tugged off and she blinked in the late day sunshine. She sat in an open glade of tangled grass and wildflowers, surrounded by a high wall of thorn. The heavy air smelled of pine and honeysuckle.

Large stones, as big as a man, stood at cardinal points around the edge of the glade. There were icons chiseled into their flat faces, a different one for each stone. Evelyn didn't recognize the sigils.

A score of people fussed with a supply cart. They wore sturdy, utilitarian clothes, and swords hung from their hips. Soldiers? There was tension in the air, and they moved quickly, placing rocks in a ring around the cart. Evelyn saw these were identical to the large rocks, facing out rather than in. A block within a block. They were hiding from the three approaching Evelyns.

A black-haired child stared at her until someone smacked him and shoved a fat pillow into his arms. He hurriedly placed the pillow on the long grass in front of her while a soldier carefully lifted an ancient man from the back of the cart.

As the old man was carried to the pillow, he watched Evelyn sharply with his good eye, while his other, opaque eye turned away. His beard was wispy, and his skin was starkly white.

"Evelyn Aeterna," he rasped. One of his legs stuck out awkwardly, the knee seemingly locked into place.

"Thurious?" she said, surprised.

"You recognize me."

"Of course," she said. "Our fight was only a few minutes ago—for me. How much time has passed? Forty years?"

"Nearer to fifty. I have aged."

She appraised him. He seemed calm, but she sensed a nervous eagerness in him. "How many times have you sat across from me?"

His eyebrows quirked up. "Ah. So you're one of the clever ones."

"Clever ones?"

He smiled and adjusted his leg. "Different pieces, different personalities. There are emotional ones and cold ones; courageous and cowardly ones." He gestured at her. "Stupid ones and clever ones."

"I don't feel like a splintered bit of myself." She looked at her bound hands, and her heart beat slowly. "I must just feel like this piece of my personality has always felt."

"Very clever."

"How many times have you brought me here over the years?" she asked again firmly.

"Many times," he said. "More than thirty. It's hard to beat your sisters to arriving fragments, but we have our methods."

"Sisters?" She looked at the stones that blocked her from sensing the other Evelyns, and it bothered her that these stones had power over her.

"Three," he said. "The eldest two are made up of over a hundred fragments by now, one more than the other. The third is more recent, about ten years old. Clever like you. I'd guess she's made up of about thirty fragments, and she's quick. If she had more time and there were more fragments remaining, she might overtake the others." He shook his head. "She arrived out of the blue one day, evaded the other two until she could get established, and has been skirting the edges of the fight ever since. I'd love to know what makes her different, but we're not on speaking terms."

"What fight?"

"Your sisters war constantly."

Evelyn mulled over this, aware that it was essentially she whom he was talking about. "Whose sigils are those?" She gestured at the standing stones with her bound hands. "It's like nothing you invoked during the civil war."

"It's not important." He smiled and Evelyn bristled.

"It's extremely important. If you don't know whose power you borrow, then you're a fool. Are they demons, or gods?"

"Whose power do *you* borrow? Where did you get your immortality?"

"Is that what you seek? Maybe I was born of the mists."

"You're not divine. I've killed enough of you to know you bleed like any other, and I weary of this conversation."

"And yet you still have it."

"Five hundred and fifty years ago you arrived at the hall of Prince Aethryt of the Thrush Clan, already a powerful mage and already ageless, but you didn't just arise from the mist. You're too mortal for that. Who were you before?" He gestured at the inscribed standing stones. "Who did you sell your soul to for immortality?"

Evelyn narrowed her eyes. Her 'memories' of those early days were long gone. "I never make contracts with demons."

"Tell me." His fingers danced an angry pattern.

Evelyn recognized his truth spell, and she jerked as it took hold of her.

She remembered playing with a wooden mallet and balls under a blossoming cherry tree. There were other girls there. It was a birthday party. But she also knew that cherry trees had not been introduced to the kingdom until the treaty of Gramanpary. She'd helped craft that treaty two hundred years ago.

"No!" Thurious said firmly.

Evelyn remembered sitting in council with a young version of King Aldus IV. This memory was not old. Maybe a hundred years.

"Again," came Thurious' voice.

Evelyn felt a harder spell hit like a migraine, felt her body topple. He was burrowing deeper.

She sat with other students in a stone schoolroom. She was a boy, which felt odd, and a mop of brown hair fell over her eyes. There were red banners on the walls. The sky outside was bitter gray. The boy daydreamed of a warmer place where he could be important.

Then it vanished and Evelyn returned to the long grass with her head pounding from the intrusion.

Thurious sighed. "Never anything useful," he said. "You've hidden your origins well, Aeterna, but I'll have them eventually."

Evelyn rubbed her neck as the ropes bit into her wrists, then pushed herself back up. "Not today," she said, wondering where such memories came from.

"Get me in the inner circle," Thurious said to his minder, who lifted him from the pillow.

"I may be your last chance," she called.

"You're not the last fragment."

"There are precious few left."

Evelyn stood slowly, legs shaking, keeping an eye on a man just behind her. It was awkward with bound ankles, but she gained her full height, taller than the minder who carried Thurious. "Where is Princess Angrassa?"

Thurious' lips pulled up into a brief sneer that melted back into a blank expression. "She's dead, fifty years gone. A death strike from your fingers as her spell took you."

Evelyn remembered casting that desperate spell. So she'd killed her last apprentice? "What a waste."

"Don't get all weepy," he snapped. "That was a long time ago and I've had this wearisome conversation with you too many times."

"Do I ever blame you?"

"Always, but I am deaf to your accusations." He waved his hand at the man behind Evelyn. "Kill her and bring me her liver and heart. You! Inner circle, now!"

Evelyn used the magic she'd been gathering for the past few hours to snap her leg-binds, then bolted. Weak as she was, the nearest standing stone was not far, and her captors were taken off guard. Still, she only led her pursuit by half a step when she passed the rock and ran straight into the thorns.

Instantly her connection with her other three selves surged to life. Close! As close as she'd hoped. The northern Evelyn was searching for her; the other two were coming quickly. The man grabbed her by the yellow dress, yanking her painfully out of the thorns, hurling her sprawling back into the circle. It was too late.

The ring of bushes violently flattened, and the standing stones cracked through their chiseled glyphs. Another Evelyn, dressed in a sturdy hunting dress, looking vibrant, strode into the panicking clearing. Her hands were up and spells of violence curled and smoked from her fingertips. There were cries and the sharp report of explosions. Horses screamed. Evelyn covered her face against flying dirt.

Thurious's minder struggled with him across the beaten glade, but Evelyn's twin gestured, and he staggered. Evelyn pushed herself to her feet and joined her other self. She could feel the other two Evelyns drawing close like thunderclouds.

"I'd forgotten about that horrid, yellow dress," her other said, looking down at it as they walked through the long grass toward the hobbling man holding Thurious.

"Are you going to absorb me?" Evelyn asked.

"Can't. We're inharmonic. All the fragments emerging from the time stream must be aligned before uniting. It's what drove our older sisters mad."

Evelyn stopped in front of Thurious. "Can we align them?"

"Only you can. You still have a connection to the temporal magic. I inherited other aspects of our old magic, not all of them useful."

"How do you know that?"

"You told me. You made me after all… you will make me. Let's handle this first." She shot Thurious a look as he glanced between the two Evelyns. "You and I have not met directly," she said to him, "though you've met many of my others. I've heard you were savage in your murders. Did our livers tell you anything?"

He shook his head, bewildered. "I've delved deeply into your memories, but there's nothing there. I've used the most powerful revelatory magic on your livers but can't find your source." His gaze fell. "It makes no sense."

While her twin studied him, Evelyn looked at her twin, fascinated. Is this how she appeared to others? She was intimidating.

"For fifty years you've been trying to steal our immortality, but this couldn't have been the way you planned it. Did something go wrong?"

"Of course something went wrong," he snapped. "You were supposed to be divided into one hundred equal portions. The fragments would emerge one at a time, and we'd handle you."

"Handle us?"

"Instead you splintered into hundreds of fragments of unequal size, scattered like a fistful of gravel into a pond."

"Why would Angrassa agree to this?"

"She hated you, Evelyn Aeterna, make no mistake."

"She didn't!"

"You took her throne."

"I had to!"

"And this is the outcome of your choices." Thurious nodded over their shoulders. "Step quickly or they'll absorb you."

Evelyn and her twin turned to see two twisted women limping into the sunlight. Evelyn braced herself to feel horror, but instead she felt a surge of pity and grief. These emotions were echoed in her twin.

She'd expected the pain, the misshapen bodies like badly stitched dolls, and the raging frustration. She didn't expect the brute confusion and yawning need to be whole. She didn't expect the helplessness. Every fragment was there in contention.

They began to lope toward her across the grass.

"Get us into the time stream," Evelyn said urgently, grabbing her twin's arm as Thurious cried "Run!" and his minder bolted. "Pull them in with us."

"You have to direct me. I can't control temporal magic."

Fighting the urge to unite with her twin, Evelyn opened her mind while the two feral ones bore down on them. Her other supplied the power, and she used it to slip the bindings of this place and enter the river of time.

The grassy glade paled and trembled, lurching forward and backward in time as they rocked in the river. Evelyn watched the waters rush by. There were fragments of herself sleeping around her. Thirty-two of them, all that was left from the original spell.

Her tortured sisters struggled and yelled as Evelyn turned to them. Was there rational thought left? What had they endured? They could be her, and she was free only by sheer luck. The first had incorporated over a hundred fragments, and the second nearer to two hundred.

"What do I do?" she asked her twin. "I can't align them when they're fighting themselves so hard."

The other Evelyn squeezed her hand. "Refragment them. Do you remember Princess Angrassa's spell?"

"Yes."

Evelyn recreated Angrassa's spell on the lesser of her two sisters, erasing the bonds that glued her together. The woman disintegrated like a dandelion puff releasing seeds onto the wind. Slowly the pieces harmonized within the river and Evelyn gathered them back together. A pure Evelyn floated before them; eyes closed. She repeated the process with the second, greater sister.

"What a hell of a thing to go through," she said. "I don't know if they'll remember anything."

"I hope they remember nothing," her twin said. "I don't want those memories when we reunite."

"We have to create you, too."

"We do."

It wasn't hard to gather the last fragments from the river. Soon, a conglomerate of herself stood before them thirty-two strong—a twin in a yellow dress. She was harmonic.

She blinked at them, confused. This was her awakening, and for her the battle for the castle had just ended. They talked to her, explained what had happened, and she understood. She was one of the clever ones after all, and with thirty-two fragments, she was not weak. She possessed modest magical powers that would grow over time.

"So you're me," the new one said to Evelyn's twin beside her.

"Yes, I'm you ten years from now. I remember this conversation, standing where you stand."

"It's all bound together, isn't it? I'll see you soon." She gave a warm smile.

Evelyn guided her newformed twin back a fraction, the smallest that she could. The woman sank into the black and rushing waters.

Evelyn sat in dew-damp grass on a hillside, mutely watching the dawn grow. Her twin sat beside her, chin on her knees. Behind them, their transformed sisters slept on the grass as perhaps they had not in years.

Below, sprawled across the valley in the predawn, lay abandoned Verginum. They knew it well. They'd seen it swell from a village to a trading hub after the royal highway was built, and then on to claim the mantle of city when the university opened and King Aldors III built his winter palace here. And now it lay abandoned. The growing light of dawn limned it.

"There's the university clock tower," said Evelyn of the silhouette. "It doesn't look damaged." Little seemed destroyed, just abandoned to time and the elements. Trees and scrub grass grew everywhere.

"The country survives," her twin said. "The battles between those two were concentrated here. It's where most of the fragments fell out. I haven't travelled south, but the Senate moved the capital to Sharash. Trade followed and the people followed after. There are towns there that blossomed. Do you remember Dillsay?"

"That little village where I pretended to be a fisher-girl?"

"It stretches along the river on both sides now, with little bridges between the two."

"I never would have imagined."

"Up here in the north there are still villages, but forests reclaimed the Thrush Valleys. Good hunting, I hear. Once our sisters began fighting, Thurious couldn't maintain his throne. The north grew wild." She waved her hand back toward the woods. "That was the last of his army."

Evelyn looked down on the royal highway that passed not far from where they sat. Its once grand width had been reduced to that of a cart path.

"Look," she said, pointing. Lights had appeared in windows, mostly on the east side of the city. Candles and cook-fires. "Verginum isn't completely dead." On the brightening plain below them, a dark cluster of tents and wagons sprang to life with movement and cook-fires of their own. A trading party.

Her twin glanced back at their sleeping selves. "Why do you think we're immortal?"

"I don't know."

"Did we just appear one day, sauntering in out of the mist? Turning a tiny country into an empire? Growing stronger each time we were killed?"

They took hands and Evelyn again felt an urge to join her. "Maybe we are divine."

"At least the loop involving me is closed. I've been created by you, gone back in time, returned to this place to rescue you, and helped send me back again. There's a beginning and an end."

"No more fragments."

"Except we four."

"There are still so many open loops though, aren't there? Bits without beginnings and ends." Understanding washed over Evelyn, and she sat up. "We could send ourselves back."

"Who, them?"

"All of us. Think about it. You appeared out of nowhere ten years ago when we sent you back, and Thurious was at his wits end to figure out where you'd come from. But it's happened before. Five hundred and fifty years ago I appeared out of the mist, and no one could explain it."

"We appeared out of nowhere." She frowned. "That's an uncomfortable loop. We'd leap back to the start, then do it over and over forever?"

"That qualifies us for divine, if nothing else," Evelyn said sarcastically.

"I don't want to have to put the kingdom back together again, or die, or get fragmented again," her twin said. "Though I don't remember any of it so it would all seem new. I'm just tired of friends growing old and dying."

Evelyn gazed at the waking Verginum. "It's why we stopped making friends."

Her twin put her chin back on her knees. "How do you think we resurrected ourselves? That's not part of any magic I know." She wiggled her fingers in an imitation of magic.

"I must have devised a resurrection spell during our First Incarnation."

"But I didn't write it down in my journal and forgot about doing it when my memory was lost? Then somehow managed to pull the same inimitable trick a century later? And why did I come back stronger each time? You don't get something from nothing. I should have come back diminished. Something else happened."

"Our dying is a powerful event at a fixed place. We could go look."

"It would take a lot of energy."

"Between the three of you we have enough."

Her twin stood and swiped dew-damp grass from her legs. "Then let's do it."

Evelyn drew her twin and sleeping sisters back into the river where all was quiet and there were no fragments of an older Evelyn to mar the surface.

"We cause such a disturbance," her twin said, watching ripples spread out around them.

"It's useless to control time. It always corrects manipulations and there are consequences."

"We're a consequence."

While they spoke, Evelyn brought them back through the decades and centuries as Verginum shrank before them from a city to a large town to a trading hub on a crossroads.

"Here!" she and her twin both said at the same time, feeling the shock of her second death near the capitol. It was an anchor, something she could locate precisely.

They emerged one hundred and ninety years ago, floating above ten thousand tents and horses. The Dilernum siege. Historians wrote that the Dilernum mages, Russef in particular, had poisoned the water supply and bottled-up Evelyn and her council for weeks until Evelyn escaped through the sewers. She'd fought Dilernum's mages face-to-face on the field, killing many, only to be killed by Russef himself.

"He really was marvelous," Evelyn said, watching him duel with her older self on the blasted, smoking plain. His reflexes were extraordinary, even seen from a distance. "He was better than I'd ever been."

"Maybe better than my second incarnation," her twin corrected, "but I returned from the dead stronger. This is hard to watch."

Evelyn knew what she meant. Her death was coming. She consoled herself that it had already happened and wouldn't be the end.

Evelyn on the battlefield, buffeted by Russef in front and a dozen wizards behind, made a magnificent showing before collapsing to her knees. Russef pounced, bowling her over, setting her alight. He followed, standing over her body, striking again and again until she was a smoking ruin. Triumphant, he turned back to the city, ordering his wizards to follow.

Evelyn waited. The body lay pitiful and small as Russef walked away. "Why am I not resurrecting myself?"

"What if I didn't? What if I can't?" her twin said. The body didn't have a head anymore, just mush like a smashed pumpkin. "We need to put one of us in her place."

Evelyn looked back at her sleeping sisters, feeling cold. "*That's* how we came back from the dead?"

"We're not immortal."

She wasn't immortal and never had been. She could die. Evelyn was shaken and saw by the ghosts behind her twin's eyes that she was too.

"Now we know why our memory was lost." Evelyn drew the stronger of her two sleeping sisters forward, the one with the greatest number of fragments. "It has to be her, because we increased in strength after we died."

She began to shake her sister's arm. "Hey," she said, "there's a man who's killed you. He's close. His back is turned. Strike quickly. Save the kingdom."

"The kingdom?" the groggy woman muttered.

"Keep the kingdom safe."

"And when you meet Thurious?" her twin added, "Kill him."

"Thurious?"

"So that's why I'll hate him so much."

They laid the woman on the blasted dirt and Evelyn hefted up what was left of the old body, drawing it back into hiding. "What a terrible mess," she said, letting it go to float idly on the river of time.

Evelyn below, beginning the third incarnation in her long life, staggered to her feet. In moments her attention fastened on the retreating back of Russef and she launched her only attack, a spear-pointed kinetic attack that ripped through the shields between his shoulder blades, punching out his spine and heart in a geyser of blood. His wizards spun at the assault and fell to their knees in terror.

"She'll be okay," Evelyn said. She vaguely remembered this part. The wizards of the city had burst out to support her, and thus had begun several years of rehabilitation as she tried to find her memories and relearn who she was. "Let's go fix another death."

The trio moved back another two hundred years, to when Evelyn was first killed. A personal betrayal. An aging lover, manipulated by factions arrayed against her. The country was awash in a religious revival with priests calling her a demon.

Historians marked this moment as the beginning of the end of the temple's independent power. Through Evelyn's first one hundred and fifty years, she and the temple had coexisted uneasily. Killing her brought the conflict to a head.

Below them, a group of gray-robed priests moved quickly along a forest road. Two horses pulled a cart with a body in bloody linen. Evelyn's body. They'd taken her by surprise when she was with her lover. Now they were returning the body to the castle to display.

"We woke up in that linen," Evelyn's twin said.

"We sat up and told them their god wasn't strong enough. That's what the histories say."

"I'll go down there."

"No, we increased in power each time we died. It has to be her, not you. She's over a hundred fragments."

"I don't want to be the first incarnation, to die like that. That'll be my body down there. Me."

Evelyn could hear the strain in her twin's voice and drew her into a tight hug. "The first incarnation was the most exciting. A dozen minor kings vying for power, borders that shifted daily, the Joshites building temples everywhere while the Hurites kept burning them down."

"There was famine too. Six years of bad winters and cool summers."

"You get to start the legend. Don't think how it ends."

"Why don't *you* become the first incarnation then?"

"Because I'm only one fragment. I'm here because I can manipulate time."

Evelyn pulled their sleeping sister forward. "You're going to wake up in bindings," she called into her sister's ear. "It's okay. The priests think they've killed you. When they open the bindings, kill the ones wearing the fanciest robes. Then declare you're stronger than their god."

"That's a lot to remember," her twin said.

"It'll work out. She's nearly three times as strong as you, after all. She'll defend herself."

With a quick slip, they tugged off her ragged clothes and switched their sister with the naked body on the cart. The priestly party moved on, oblivious.

"One last place to go," her twin said quietly. "There's no anchor this time to guide us. Just appear about a hundred and fifty years ago, and that'll be the day I arrived. Hey, be careful with her, that's me!"

Evelyn released the corpse onto the river as she had with the body of the second incarnation. "Do you want to say some final words?"

"Let's just go."

And so they moved to a time before the kingdom. Prince Aethryt had been declared king of the Thrush Clan in a quick ceremony after his father was killed in battle against the Gurret Clan. The situation for the Thrush was dire.

"It's muddy," her twin said, looking at her boots. Thick fog draped the growing dawn.

"Everything is muddy. The ground... the world." Evelyn looked around. She could only see about thirty feet in any direction. The trunks of pines stood like ghosts. Waking birds sounded muffled.

"We need good roads. The lanes stringing together the villages are probably infested with highwaymen. Wolves too."

"They can't imagine the peace we'll bring."

Her twin held out a hand. "Shall we unite?"

"No." It took a force of will for Evelyn to resist that offer. "I want to head back to our fragmentation to see what Angrassa really did, and then make sure Thurious doesn't cause more problems."

Her twin didn't seem surprised. "If you need help, go to Jonathan. Do you remember him? The Hammer who survived?"

"Of course I do."

"He commanded the army after Senator Kouler was killed. He's head of the Senate now, though he's ancient. With Thurious and all the Evelyns gone, he'll want to return north."

Evelyn stared down the muddy forest track. "I can't picture him as a gristled leader."

"People surprise you. What'll you do after that? They don't need us anymore."

"They haven't needed us in a hundred years. Maybe I'll have an adventure. Maybe I'll age."

Her twin looked down the lane with her. They'd both heard a creak of leather. "I'm certain that growing old isn't as exciting as it sounds. We have company."

"Thrush, or one of the other clans?"

"No idea. They didn't exactly wear uniforms this far back." Shapes moved among the trees. Men in grays and browns and blacks; men with swords bound for silence. "We're lucky they're wearing clothes at all."

"I'm guessing they're not Thrush."

"They've seen you. It's that damned yellow dress."

Evelyn hugged her tightly. "I'd say good luck, but we know how this ends."

"It ends with me dead on a cart and you stealing my body." She grimaced. "I wonder how many times we've done this."

"It's how we got so strong. We keep increasing in power, being sundered, and doing it all over. Give me a push?" Her twin magically shoved her back into the river of time and then raised her hands against the invading men.

How many times *had* they done this? It must have had a beginning somewhere.

As she slipped forward in time and cities blossomed around her, Evelyn instantly missed her twin. She'd been alone for five hundred years, and now she was leaving her sister to die. She wrapped her arms around herself tightly.

Her fragmentation quickly approached, and she slowed her forward drift. Thurious and Angrassa's forces assaulted the capital and poured through the narrow streets. The castle burned and towers collapsed, taking rooms and halls and countless people with them. Evelyn moved down familiar corridors to the old throne room, remaining in the river but slowing her drift until she matched the pace of time in the world. She obscured herself in shadows and floated near the room's heavy rafters, half in the river, half out. The large space below her was lit by the glow of flames through the stained-glass windows.

In the silence before the coming fight, it surprised her that she grieved. She'd lived so long and buried so many that grief was rare. It was gratifying that Jonathan had survived and flourished, but what about all the others dying on this night? Could she help save them? She didn't have much magical strength.

Men and women wearing red entered below her with armfuls of candles. Princess Angrassa limped in after them wearing white, favoring her shortened leg, ordering the candles lit. She positioned them this way and that around the room's edges, and Evelyn realized from her elevated perch that the candles were part of a spell, laid out in a staccato configuration which she'd missed when she burst into the room. It looked like a mathematical variant of an imprisonment spell.

So Angrassa had not been performing a premature coronation when Evelyn arrived. She'd been laying a trap.

Thurious appeared in a bloody uniform. Angrassa looked up at him and a cold expression seized her face.

"You're not ready? They're pushing her this way; she could be here at any moment!"

"She's over by that big planet and sun model," he said, sounding exhausted. Evelyn grew ashamed of how easily they'd manipulated her.

"The Orrery," Angrassa snapped. "Go get changed."

He stared. "I've been fighting! We had to invade first, remember?"

Angrassa turned away. "How's she going to get around the library fire if she's still at the Orrery?"

"I have people putting out the fire. If she can't get through that way, we'll herd her through the kitchens. She'll blunder into the royal wing eventually."

Angrassa nodded tersely. "I'll set up background magic, so she's drawn to us. Where are the Hammers? We need Hammers to batter her shields."

"They're coming. I had to use more of them than I wanted to get you safe passage through. The Senate put up strong resistance."

She flicked her hand in dismissal. "That was because of Evelyn Aeterna. The Senate will be disbanded tomorrow as my first order."

"I thought your first order was to make me king."

"You can't be king if there's a senate, can you?"

Evelyn was surprised at the hardness in Angrassa's tone, and the frustration in his. The princess was not the demure ingénue she'd pretended to be, and theirs was not a lovebird infatuation.

Evelyn had been played for a fool.

"Where's my chair!?" Angrassa snapped.

Men hurried forward with a cloth-wrapped chair; the chair Evelyn had assumed was from the dining gallery. Angrassa unwound it and turned it upside-down. Evelyn grew angrier because the underside of the chair was covered in script, similar to what Thurious had carved into the standing stones fifty years hence. Angrassa ran her finger along the etched symbols.

Thurious reappeared in the door wearing a clean uniform.

"She's coming," he said. "We lost her going through the library fire, but she's in the royal wing now."

"Everyone get where you're supposed to be!" Angrassa flipped the chair over. "Do not step out of position, no matter what happens. You there, attack her when she comes through the door—take her by surprise."

Evelyn noted that the people on the dais were not standing in a random configuration. It was a geometric spell. It was an amplification configuration, usually done with quartz crystals on pedestals. What was Angrassa trying to do? She sat in the focal point, perched on her scribed chair. The man she'd selected to attack Evelyn stood to the side, out of the configuration. He was sacrificial and he knew it. He was trembling.

Evelyn's eyes returned to the candlelit barrier. What was it for? It could keep a spell contained, but it was useless as a physical trap.

And then the target arrived. Evelyn Aeterna, she of the Third Incarnation, stamping around with false bravado to intimidate those on the dais, oblivious to the trap.

The sacrificial Hammer attacked, and Evelyn Aeterna killed him without hesitation. The crowd jumped. Angrassa assumed a frightened expression and Thurious assumed a bluster as Evelyn Aeterna mocked them. All the while, Evelyn above watched energy flowing from the people into Angrassa's chair. The princess was stealing the strength of her Hammers through the augmentation geometry. It was an evil thing.

Four Hammers attacked together, and Evelyn Aeterna turned aside their assault. Evelyn above saw the wince on Angrassa's face and the glance by Thurious, but Evelyn Aeterna was focused on the Hammers and didn't see.

She circled, and the people on the dais turned with her like puppets. The link between Angrassa's chair and their bodies pulsed.

Another Hammer attacked. Evelyn Aeterna killed him, and the crowd broke and ran. A look of panic crossed the princess' face as the magic being drawn into her chair vanished.

Evelyn Aeterna threw a caustic attack which Thurious barely deflected.

Angrassa stood, one of her legs hooked around the chair leg while Evelyn Aeterna challenged Thurious. The energy in the chair burst up into the princess' body and she hurled out all that magic in one impressive assault.

Evelyn Aeterna slung the final killing spell before Angrassa's attack struck her, driving her back. Evelyn's spirit shredded into a hundred pieces and Evelyn above winced in kindred pain. Below, Evelyn's last killing spell ricocheted off Angrassa's defenses and hit Thurious, driving him to the floor.

Princess Angrassa leaned on her glowing chair while Evelyn Aeterna's soul-fragments rose in a swirling ascent, tumbling around the circle of candles. Angrassa spell-shouted into the maelstrom and her ensorcelled chair shook violently. She remained safe in its protection.

Evelyn above couldn't let this continue. But as she gathered her small magical capabilities, Princess Angrassa suddenly flopped back onto her chair, jaw hanging slack. Her breathing stopped and a glow of energy surrounded her. Evelyn gaped at the audacity. Angrassa was transferring her soul from her body into Evelyn Aeterna's corpse. This was the heart of her spell.

It *was* all about the immortality! As with Thurious in the future, Angrassa was trying to steal what she could not create. And she might succeed. If Evelyn Aeterna's body was still unhinged from time, it would remain ageless.

Redirecting the magic she'd gathered; Evelyn created a weak shield in front of Evelyn Aeterna's body just as Angrassa's soul made the leap between corporeal forms. With a cry that shivered down Evelyn's spine, Angrassa's soul rebounded and was snatched into the swirling cascade of Evelyn-fragments sweeping around the circle. The Princess was torn apart. Evelyn's one hundred fragments smashed back and forth, combining, splintering, multiplying. Thurious sat on the floor, his knee shattered, one eye burned opaque, and laughed.

But Angrassa was not defeated. Evelyn above watched her reconstitute much of her soul by force of will, and with a vibrant groan tried to dive back into her old body. She rebounded as she had from Evelyn's shield, this time blocked by her own protections in the chair, and instead crashed down into Thurious. He convulsed, his soul ejected like a paint splatter, which was yanked up into the howling tumult at the ceiling.

Angrassa, now inside Thurious' crippled body, fought to a sitting position and raised his hands, fingers flashing. Evelyn saw that she was again attempting the transfer to Evelyn Aeterna.

Evelyn above closed her fist and a single candle snuffed out. Fragments instantly poured through the gap in a churning rush. Princess Angrassa, stuck in Thurious' body, stared dumbfounded.

Unprepared for the deluge, Evelyn above couldn't dodge and was pierced by a score of fragments and hurled back into the river of time.

Evelyn walked through the twilit pine forest fifty years hence, approaching Thurious' glade from the opposite side of where she and her young twin were just leaving. Her body ached with the languor of utter exhaustion. Her yellow dress snagged on thorns, and she tugged it free absentmindedly. She really needed something else to wear.

She didn't have to wait long for Thurious and his minder to come barreling through the trees. Their footsteps thumped against the carpet of pine needles.

"Hello," Evelyn called.

The man carrying Thurious came up short, breathing hard.

"How did you get ahead of us?" Thurious demanded. "Which one are you?"

"Has there ever needed to be more than one of me?" She smiled. "I've travelled far since we last spoke... Princess."

Thurious' eyes narrowed sharply as his gnarled fingers burst into motion. "I *will* kill you, no matter how many times it takes."

Evelyn didn't shield against the new-forming spell, but instead blocked the parasitic connection between Angrassa and the man carrying her.

Angrassa gasped and arched her back in shock when the source of her energy snapped. Her minder retched and staggered, then pushed Thurious' body from him with a cry. He stared down at the writhing old man for a moment before looking at Evelyn, then raced off through the trees.

Evelyn crouched next to the old man. "You don't look well." She guessed something had broken in Angrassa's fall. Maybe ribs.

Angrassa's face contorted. "Who gave it to you?!" she gasped. "And don't give me that bullshit about being divine. Who granted you immortality?"

Evelyn laughed. "Maybe you can raise another broken memory from me."

Angrassa's eyes tightened. "Those were my memories!"

"I know. You lost part of your soul to me, didn't you? And I have some of Thurious' memories too."

"Yes."

"I don't have all of him," Evelyn said, touching her chest, "so his soul didn't stay with me. What happened to him?"

"A bunch of him reappeared in a clump early on, but you'd wounded him badly. Whenever he appeared he died without a fuss, so I stopped keeping track of him."

Anger roiled Evelyn's stomach. Several of the final fragments that had joined with her were of Thurious. "Why didn't you move to a new body after that night? Why grow old?"

"I couldn't anymore!" Angrassa cried, then dropped her head to the dirt. "I lost too much of my soul to you. I couldn't do the magic."

"*Anymore*? You did it before?"

Angrassa peered up at her. "You trained me to be ambitious, but after you made me queen, you blocked me at every turn. You never allowed me to rule."

"You weren't queen." An odd memory of being an aging queen suddenly surfaced in Evelyn's mind.

"Not here," Angrassa said. "In my own time I reigned for fifty years, and we clashed every day I sat on the throne."

Evelyn sat back on her heels, stunned.

"I mastered temporal magic to seek out your origins," Angrassa continued, "but you discovered me, and we fought. You thought you'd killed me. I escaped with my dying breath. Sent my soul back to inhabit my twenty-year old body, then I attacked you. I took you by surprise. That time I thought I had you, but you *would not die*. I had to escape again, this time to my fifteen-year-old self. I was going to take your body with that transfer spell. I was finally going to be rid of you!"

Evelyn remembered the dramatic change in the fifteen-year-old princess, right when Thurious arrived at court. Maybe if she hadn't been so focused on him she might have seen Angrassa's true nature. She was in awe of the magic Angrassa had manipulated.

"You can't change time," she said softly, speaking as much to herself as to the princess. "It corrects itself. You reigned for fifty years in both timelines, and now here we are."

"I hate you!"

The killing spell that erupted from Angrassa's fingers was unexpectedly powerful, backed by two lifetimes of bitter obsession. Evelyn barely raised shields, and they crackled and flared under the onslaught. She couldn't withstand it for long, so she snatched up a heavy branch and swung it across Angrassa's temple. Then again and again with increasing fury. She hurled the branch aside, chest heaving, and turned her back on the corpse. The birds and insects in the darkening woods had fallen silent.

She looked down at her arms. Blood spattered them up to her elbows.

She had killed a great many people over the centuries, but never by hand. Always through distancing magic. And except for Russef, always with an overwhelming advantage.

She looked back to the body. "*You* made me immortal when you cast me onto the river of time," she said softly.

Loneliness settled on her like a weight. She had no birth! She'd always clung to the belief that she had a childhood somewhere, buried in the forgotten past. Instead, every five hundred years she fragmented and recombined with chunks of Angrassa's and

Thurious' souls in an awful dance. She was born from them, if you could call it that. They were her mother and father. Angrassa's ambition to rule was Evelyn's ambition.

She stepped wearily over crushed thorn bushes into the washed-out twilight of the glade, stepping around bodies. Thurious' last soldiers. She looked at their faces. They had names, surely. Men and women who hadn't been alive at the start of this and hadn't survived until its end.

She'd killed them without thought. Her twin had actually done it, but she could have. Any one of her would have done the same. She was as much a killer as Angrassa. Queen Angrassa. She rubbed at the blood on her arms, numb.

Angrassa's supply cart stood at the forest's edge with nervous horses still in the traces. Evelyn knew with heightened senses that the young boy who'd carried Thurious' pillow cowered in the back.

She approached the cart slowly, thinking maybe she'd go south to Jonathan and the Senate. She imagined a grand entrance, walking the length of the senate floor with her head high before the shocked senators. She'd wrap herself in the cloak of her own legend and tell them the north was safe. She would be Evelyn Aeterna once more.

It would be a moment for the historians. Her saga would have an ending, even if there was no beginning.

"Boy," she called to the cart. "Come help me with the horses. I won't hurt you."

About the Author

Jeffrey Lyman has been writing for as long as he can remember, typically doorstop epic fantasies that originally didn't go anywhere and just trailed off, to later efforts that actually went somewhere. He has found he has a knack for keeping all the spinning plates aloft until it's time for them to start falling. His short stories have been published a baker's dozen times in several award-winning anthologies, as well as assisting in editing, and he attended the Odyssey Writing Workshop in 2004. Professionally, he was published in Orson Scott Card's Intergalactic Medicine Show, as well as winning Writers of the Future in 2010 (published 2011). After that, he took a hiatus to raise a family. With the boys being fifteen and sixteen now, and more interested in video games than hanging out with Dad, he has once again taken up the pen. He recently published a steampunk novelette in the anthology *The Chaos Clock*, by eSpec Books, which was delightfully reviewed in Tangent Online.